FIRESIGN

A Detective LaFleur Mystery

Steve Abbott

——

John Fountain

To Adrienne and Sandy
(again and always)

Forward

In Oswego in 1998, a young woman tragically died in a fire in an apartment on Bridge Street. The fire is generally considered to have been arson, which makes her death a murder, no matter the original intention of the arsonist.

No one has ever been charged.

The fire had a local signature. Someone must have seen something; must have heard something; must know something.

New York is a death penalty state. There is no statute of limitations on murder.

Someone knows.

Firesign

Prologue

Amy woke up coughing.

She got out of bed and started to stand up, but quickly dropped to her hands and knees; the room was full of smoke.

"Robbie!" she cried. No, wait, Robbie's not here tonight.

She crawled towards the kitchen, where in the dim light she saw smoke crawling thick and dark across the floor, a cheap stage effect. A thin stream of smoke flowed rapidly up the wall and out through the kitchen window, partially open to the summer night air.

She crab-walked back out of the kitchen to the front of the small apartment. As she grabbed the door handle she dimly registered that it was hot, hot enough that she reflexively pulled her hand away, but she didn't get a chance to think about it for long.

The door blew open with an odd rushing sound, and a wall of fire washed over her like a wave.

CHAPTER 1

"Ohmygod." Maggie gasped and clutched her hands to her throat, arms tight across her chest, in a cold flush of shock. She had never, in her forty years of nursing, seen a burn victim this bad before. Actually, she had never seen *anything* this bad before. Maggie had had more than her share of experience with burns, but this was not something even her years of experience had prepared her for.

The burn blanket that had covered the girl during transport to the burn unit shifted slightly as she was moved into the E.R, revealing a patchwork of sterile dressings, raw burned areas, and blackened flaps of nightgown stuck to burned flesh. The smell was nearly overpowering—an acrid mix of burnt hair and charred meat. There was an IV tube attached to one arm, the needle poked into a mottled, puffy mass, now barely held in place by a wrapping of gauze. There was another IV as well, Maggie saw, an intraosseous line in her tibia—they're pumping fluids into her as fast as they can, she thought. The girl's head was covered with a wet dressing, one singed, blond braid visible, lying on the sterile sheet beside her, like a summer camp craft project, a lanyard, a small belt. Her face was swollen and just as raw under the thin strips of gauze as the rest of her upper body. The EMTs had her on oxygen, of course, using a nasal cannula. A mask would not have worked, and intubation will have to be done as soon as possible at the burn center.

One of the EMTs adjusted the blanket as Maggie stepped back out of the way. The girl made a small mewling sound as the gurney rolled past. Maggie's chest constricted in anguish as she realized it was an attempt to scream.

CHAPTER 2

Ex-detective A.C. LaFleur checked his cards again, forgetting whether he had two spades or if one of them was a club. That would make a difference in deciding whether to call—out of position with a moderate raise in front of him, he was not all that impressed with the strength of his hand. Especially as he saw, peering through the bottom of his glasses, that he did in fact have split suits.

He slipped his glasses off and laid them on the table on top of his cards, ran his fingers through his thick, graying hair, then leaned back with his hands behind his head. He had kept himself in shape over the winter, and had even lost a few pounds. Wintering in Florida didn't require the constant influx of calories that a long New York winter demanded, and he hadn't cut back on the amount of physical exercise he was used to. All in all, he felt great, maybe even better than before he left.

He'd been back in New York for only a few weeks, but was already comfortably resettled on the houseboat. This was the second poker game since getting back in late April, after the snow was gone off the streets and the ice in the marina cleared. He couldn't stop talking about how relieved he was to be back.

He'd sold his condo in Florida the year before. Buying it with the insurance money his wife left when she died had seemed like a good idea at the time, but he found that he couldn't relax and enjoy it. Plus a big increase in the association fees really steamed him. He had been fortunate to get out of the whole thing at break-even. The cottage in Sarasota that he had planned to rent instead had suddenly been sold for taxes, foreclosed, or fallen under some sort of mortgage crisis turnover; the long and short of it was that he had to scramble to find something at the last minute, and ended up on the wrong side of the Tamiami Trail. The house had looked reasonable enough in the pictures he was sent; it was obvious, once he got there, that the photos had been taken some years earlier.

"Bugs. Did I mention the bugs?" Yes, he had, they said. No matter. "Ants. Can't leave the sugar bowl out, they attack in barbarian hordes. Then there are things that look like cockroaches, but are too big to be cockroaches. I don't know what they are.

"And traffic. The drivers there. Pretty much a take 'em or leave 'em attitude to red lights."

"We get it, A.C.," said Michael Fuentes, chief anesthesiologist at Oswego hospital and a close friend. "But you're back in good old upstate New York now, with bugs you know and love. And we stop for red lights here. There aren't many red lights in Oswego to worry about, anyway, town or city."

16

LaFleur took the unlit cigar out of the side of his mouth to point it at Michael.

"Damn right we stop for red lights here," he said. "Law abiding citizenry. Know the rules and stick to them."

This was too much for Father Thomas Manetti—or "Father Tommy," as he preferred to be called—an old friend but a new addition to the poker regulars this year. "And which Oswego would we be talking about, then? The same Oswego I live in? And how long, exactly, have you been off the force? You've forgotten what it was like?"

"I'll allow we have our share, ok, maybe more than our share, of crime hereabouts," LaFleur admitted. "But still, when there's a problem, we deal with it. Not like Florida, where...."

"Maybe when you were on active duty, A.C. Not the same now. Nowhere near." This was from Charlie Case, who had retired from the Oswego Fire Department a couple of years earlier. "Nowhere near," he repeated.

This stopped LaFleur short for a moment, then he graciously accepted the subtle compliment. He had always prided himself on his competence as a detective. After retiring, he had been out of sorts for awhile. He missed both the challenge and the sense of accomplishment that came with resolving a tough case. But there had also been the cold case of the dead nurse that Michael and Maggie pulled him into the year before, right before LaFleur left for Florida. That had not gone as well as he would have liked.

Charlie continued, bringing LaFleur back from his reverie. "There's some things going on around here now that could use some real investigation," he said. "The fire," he said pointedly, in response to LaFleur's quizzical look. "That investigation is going nowhere fast, as usual. The DA's office and our new Chief of Police—and I use the

17

term advisedly—are stonewalling the OFD, again as usual. What is it about fires and Oswego, anyway?"

LaFleur had heard something about the recent fire but had not paid close attention. But he had to admit Charlie was right, fires seemed to be unusually popular in and around Oswego, especially in the past few years; there had been several fairly major fires in the downtown area, all suspicious, and all unsolved, as far as he knew. He was not surprised to hear Charlie complaining about the current state of law enforcement. There had been a flurry of scandals surrounding the district attorney, mayor, and police department several years earlier—one mayor had even been run out of office, and still managed to get himself elected as an alderman on the Common Council six months later—but it was generally thought that most of that was all in the past. With the exception of the current police chief, that is. LaFleur had been hearing rumblings involving the chief even before leaving for the winter.

"No different than the arson fire a few years ago, you remember that," Charlie was saying, pulling LaFleur into the conversation. LaFleur nodded. "Same kind of fire," Charlie went on, "pizza joint below a few apartments, and the same result—two college kids injured, no charges ever filed, even though everyone knew it was arson. I almost resigned over that, did you know that? No, probably not, I don't like to talk about it. I was blocked at every turn. But I'm ready to talk about it now, I'll tell you."

LaFleur knew Charlie Case well enough to know that if he was dissatisfied with whatever investigation was going on now, there was probably something to it. As Charlie continued to describe the circumstances of the most recent fire, going into the reasons he thought it was suspicious, he was obviously trying to convince him that there was more

18

to it than an accidental kitchen fire or faulty wiring. LaFleur was only half listening. The other half—the wary half—was silently vowing that he should stay out of it. He was not about to get pulled into another impossible situation, he told himself. But at the same time, it did sound intriguing.

***

The game broke up early, LaFleur uncharacteristically down a few dollars. There had been more interest in the discussion than in the game, anyway, particularly as it was just the four of them this time, not enough for a very good game— three regular players from the detective force had cancelled. Not that the stakes were going to make or break anyone, but it was a way of keeping score. Otherwise might as well play tiddlywinks. *God, that dates me,* he thought; *when's the last time you heard anyone mention tiddlywinks.* The phone rang; it was Maggie.

"Hi, Maggie," he said, answering, pleasantly surprised at hearing her voice; they had talked only the day before and he hadn't expected to hear from her again so soon. Not that he didn't want to hear from her, just that since she had moved down to Syracuse while he was away for the winter, they hadn't quite hooked up again. Not in the way it had been last fall.

His pleasure at hearing from her again so soon didn't last. She had called about the burn victim she had been caring for over the past two days.

"God, Maggie, that sounds rough," he said after listening a minute. "What's the prognosis, any chance she'll come out of it ok?"

19

He frowned at her answer. The girl was not doing well, she told him.

"Yes, of course, come on up," LaFleur answered in response to her question about seeing him. "Tomorrow night, sure. No, I don't have much on hand; we can just walk over to Patz as usual...Sure...Sure, I'm sure. How long can you stay? Ok, see you soon."

CHAPTER 3

Patz On the River sits at the south end of the Port Authority marina, on the east side of the river. Sitting somewhat away from the port loading area, the restaurant and bar both afford great views across the river to the west, and out to Lake Ontario. It is one of, if not *the* most popular spot in Oswego, and has been for several years. LaFleur's old hangout, the 1850 House over on Bridge, had closed down while he was in Florida, so on his return he shifted his social center of operations to Patz. It was an easy transition.

Pat and Pat, the husband and wife owners of Patz, ("He-Pat" and "She-Pat," as they were sometimes known, whenever it was necessary to indicate which one you were talking about) were old friends of LaFleur's, and he had spent a lot of time at Patz over the years, even if it had not been an exclusive habit.

Being so close to the marina, Patz was an easy walk from the houseboat. Too easy, at times; many nights he had lulled himself into a false sense of security, knowing how close home was, only to discover that walking along a cold, dark river in the rain after a shot or few could be not only daunting but dangerous. One particularly bad night—bad in more ways than one—he had to be given a ride around to the other side of the marina, a two-block walk. That had been some time ago; he was less extravagant in his imbibitional habits these days.

Maggie was already waiting in the parking lot late the next afternoon when LaFleur walked up. She was looking harried—she'd left work in a rush and her long, auburn hair was still tied up in a nurse's bun. He complimented her looks, and she laughed, knowing exactly how she looked. They kissed a little awkwardly and went in. LaFleur steered her to his "summer" booth, near the windows next to the bar. In cooler weather he staked out a table next to the fireplace.

"How're you doing?" he asked, as they sat down.

"Oh, I'll be alright. I just wanted to get away for a few hours."

"Can't talk you into spending the night?"

"No, I really need to get back tonight; I have an early shift tomorrow."

"Alright." They both reached out across the table at the same time; a quick squeeze and a smile to let each other know it really was all right.

"The Padre is playing poker with us now, did I tell you?" LaFleur asked, changing the subject.

Maggie smiled at the mention of Father Tommy. They had become very close during a traumatic period in

Maggie's life a few months earlier. "I'll bet he's got a great poker face."

"No kidding. He took me for about twenty bucks last night. I'm looking forward to getting it back." He let go of Maggie's hands as the waitress, Nikki Faghin, walked up.

"Hi, Nikki. Let's see, a red wine—probably don't have any Eye of the Swan back there?" He knew she did—they kept it stocked for Maggie, at LaFleur's request. "And the same for me. Still a little early for scotch yet."

"When is it ever too early for a shot of The Famous Grouse?" Nikki smiled at the name of LaFleur's favorite brand, another item stocked primarily for him. She turned her head, tilting it slightly, a nervous habit LaFleur had noticed before. "Hi, Maggie." It looked like she was going to say something else, but heard her name called and turned towards the bar. "Ok," she called out over her shoulder, then turned back and said, "Be right back, guys."

"No problem. And a couple of menus when you get a chance."

As Nikki walked away, Maggie raised an eyebrow. "Come here a lot, do you?" she said playfully.

"It beats hell out of my cooking."

"I'd have to agree."

"Not to mention the fact that her and Fuentes—oops." He smiled up at Nikki as she ducked in quickly and set two glasses of wine and a pair of menus on the table. "Thanks, Nikki."

As soon as Nikki turned and left, LaFleur pushed the menus to one side as they raised their glasses: "Health."

Maggie just nodded, looked down, than back at LaFleur, her eyes faintly glistening.

"Bad one, eh?" he said quietly. Maggie just nodded again, took a sip of wine, and then seemed to gather herself.

"She's stable—oh, her name is Amy Polwicz—but she still hasn't regained consciousness. So it's going to be a long haul. If she makes it." She paused, reflectively glancing away then back. "They're pumping Ringer's into her, not by the liter, but by the gallon," she said. "We're really not much farther along in this century than last when it comes to burns this severe. The chief surgeon has talked about some experimental methods of grafting, and she's getting a load of broad spectrum antibiotics. Family and friends have been donating blood, but…"

LaFleur was surprised to see Maggie start to tear up as her voice trailed off—he'd always thought nurses were hard as nails. "There's a 'rule of thumb' used in burn units to estimate survival rates. You take the age of the patient, and add the total burn percentage. That gives you the fatality rate. Amy is twenty years old, with eight-five percent second and third degree burns."

It didn't take LaFleur all that long to do the math. *105%. Christ.* "Any word on an arson investigation?" he asked.

"The police were down late yesterday to question her," Maggie said, recovering herself a bit. Still, LaFleur couldn't miss the disconsolation in her voice. "Of course I couldn't even let them into the ICU—I don't know why they didn't call ahead—but they told me she was the only one injured in the fire. No clue yet as to what caused it." She looked out the window. The lighthouse out at the mouth of the river was silhouetted in the falling darkness like a giant chess piece.

"Oh, yeah, I was going to tell you about seeing Charlie Case," said LaFleur, breaking the silence. "He plays poker with us now too, you know. He mentioned the fire; says he's not surprised that they haven't got anything on it yet.

He was even talking about a fire from, what, ten years ago?—eleven?—another pizza parlor fire. Said there are a lot of similarities, and that they bollixed up that investigation, just like they are now, he claims. I think he's seeing a lot of smoke where there's no fire, if you'll pardon the pun—"

"No worse than usual." She very pointedly didn't smile.

"Anyway," LaFleur forged ahead, "he didn't convince me that there was anything seriously wrong, so far at least. We'll just have to wait and see, I guess."

"God, A.C. I hope they find out what happened. Somebody should be held responsible for this. Accident or not."

"I agree, babe."

She looked at him more intently. "Nothing you can do?"

He tried a pained look, but succeeded only in looking peeved. "You can't be serious, after what happened last year?"

"That was different. And anyway, that turned out just fine in the end."

He just looked down at the table and didn't say anything more at this. As far as he was concerned, his performance the previous fall in investigating the alleged suicide of a young nurse named Angie had only proven to everyone, himself included, that he had retired from the force none too soon.

LaFleur had taken on the unofficial investigation only at Maggie's—and the Padre's—insistence, and in the end had taken it a bit too far. If it hadn't been for Michael's profound expertise in anesthesiology, along with some very quick thinking, Maggie would probably be dead now, the victim of a desperate and irrational attempt to cover up

25

evidence. And for what? The possibility that he had, maybe, remotely, accidentally, found a potential murder suspect, well, two suspects, neither of whom were ever anything more than *possible* suspects—and now, one of them dead of a heart attack and the other one missing...well, his only consolation was that there had been a small measure—very small in his opinion—of closure for some of the parties involved. He shook his head at the memory, then looked back up at Maggie.

"Let's let the department deal with this one, shall we?" LaFleur almost pleaded.

"But you just said that Charlie Case—"

"Yeah, but that's Charlie. That doesn't mean that—"

"And what about her boyfriend. Robert. Robbie. I mean, he's just devastated," she went on, interrupting him right back. "Really nice kid. He feels guilty about leaving Amy alone in the apartment, even though he knows there was nothing he could have done. He is desperate to know what happened, and doesn't see much action from the authorities. He just wants some answers at this point. You can understand that, can't you?"

"Well..."

Maggie would not be denied. "At least give Amos a call, will you?" Amos Brown was LaFleur's old partner on the force, nearing retirement himself now. "Find out where they are in this? I can't stand the thought of it being swept under the rug. Not again. Not like Angie." She set her mouth in a determined attempt to get him to see it her way. He relented.

"Ok. You're right, it can't hurt anything. And I can see that this has you pretty upset. Sorry if I'm being uncooperative. I'll call Amos first thing tomorrow."

Maggie smiled. "That's enough for now."

LaFleur waved to Nikki with his empty wine glass. "Now, can we order dinner?"

CHAPTER 4

"Had dinner with Maggie last night," LaFleur said as he and Michael slid into a booth for lunch at Patz.

"How's she doing? She's working in the Clarke burn unit down in Syracuse now, isn't she?"

LaFleur nodded. "Yeah, and they've got a bad one there now. Well, hell, you probably know about it, the girl from the fire Charlie was talking about the other day. She's in pretty bad shape, from what Maggie says."

"Well, they're good down there; Simonson's one of the best in the country. They're lucky to have him. So she should have a good chance."

"I sure hope so," LaFleur said. "Maggie's pretty shook up about it. I understand how it is, I've been shook up plenty of times. You think you know how to handle this stuff, that you've seen it all before. But then a case just hits you the wrong way, out of the blue. It's usually a little thing that triggers it, at least for me it is. Maggie was in the E.R. when they brought her in, and the way she described it, it was the sight of one of the girl's braids that somehow hadn't been burned too badly, hanging out from under the saline wraps, that really got to her. That, and a small cry the girl made as they moved her. Maggie said it just stopped her cold."

Michael was nodding in assent. "Yeah, we all get that feeling once in awhile. Hopefully not too often, or it can really get you down; but it's worse if you never feel it."

At that, Nikki flounced up, leaned over Michael's shoulder from behind and dropped a couple of menus on the table, leaving one hand resting on his shoulder. "Anything to drink today, guys?"

Nikki was as small-statured, light-toned, and bright-eyed as Michael was tall, broad and dark. With a name like "Faghin" it was only natural that Nikki looked the part of the stereotypical Irish colleen—or in Michael's words, the "Star of the County Down," the girl of the famous ballad, "nut brown" hair and all. Michael's physique and coloration—he had been born in the Dominican Republic—were an almost exact inverse. Where Nikki had skin the color of Galway milk, Michael was creamed Caribbean coffee. Nikki's eyes were bright hazel-green; Michael's were almost black. Nikki was short, about five-five, but, as LaFleur put it, "well-proportioned." Michael was a little over six feet tall and had a competition swimmer's wide shoulders and thin waist—think Michael Phelps—and chestnut-brown curly hair, which the nurses at the hospital loved running their fingers through, especially when he least expected it.

Nikki's hand started kneading the muscles running up the side of Michael's neck. "Man, you feel like you're

29

strung with steel cables today." Michael leaned into her hand a bit—it felt good—and he shook his head.

"Nothing to drink for me today, Nikki, I'm on a short leash. One of docs didn't show up today. Again."

"Nothing for me either, Nikki," said LaFleur.

Nikki patted Michael's neck as she walked away. "Ok, just wave when you're ready to order."

Michael stretched and arched his back. "Man, I could have taken another half hour of that."

"She'd be glad to oblige, I'm sure. And not stop there." He stopped short of winking.

The flush that blossomed in Michael's face was unmistakable. The cause less so, as he began to protest, in terms that left LaFleur flustered. "You know I don't go in for that kind of thing."

"That kind of thing? Just because she's a waitress? I know she has sort of a reputation…well, no, not a reputation, exactly, but anyway, Michael, I never thought you were that class-conscious."

"Oh, come off it, A.C. You know what I mean."

Actually, he didn't. But Michael didn't give him any time to pursue it.

"Tell me more about the deal with the fire and girl down in Syracuse," Michael said. "You agree with Charlie, the investigation is being botched?"

"Hell, I don't know," LaFleur answered, absently waving a hand. "I tend to trust Charlie's judgment, and he's got a hell of a lot better insight than I do into what's going on down there. The only one left I really know—and trust—is my old partner, Amos Brown. In fact, I had a long conversation with him this morning about what's going on with the fire investigation. Maggie sort of insisted." He paused and grimaced a bit at this. "So anyway, like I said, I called Amos this morning—we got to talk for quite awhile, he's stuck at a desk for a few weeks after breaking his foot in that deal down at the harbor—you hear about that?—no? well, this guy, two of them, actually, they were using this old sailboat to—"

Michael held up his hands to interrupt. "Amos is obviously a bad influence. You're starting to sound just like him. Get back to the fire investigation?"

LaFleur chuckled. "Yeah, he does go on, doesn't he? So, the fire. As much as I trust Charlie Case's instincts, Amos insists there's no evidence of arson. Fire department investigator thinks he can see where it started, in the kitchen below the apartments—probably bad wiring, and with lots of old grease behind the ovens, didn't take much of a short to set it off. Or something along those lines, anyway."

"No insurance motive? Isn't that what these things usually are? Especially around here."

"Nope. Amos interviewed the owner himself. Doesn't think he was involved. Says he feels pretty bad about the girl. And the insurance company reportedly says in their initial assessment that it was accidental. Although according to Amos they haven't sent their own investigator out yet, not as of today, anyway."

"And the girl, she was the only one injured?"

"That's right. Only two other apartments up there, they were both empty, school just being over. Amy is the girl's name. Maggie showed me a picture the family gave her. Beautiful girl. She had been sharing the apartment with a boyfriend, but he moved out a few days before, to a frat house. They questioned him and can't find any reason to think that he was involved in any way. Didn't appear to have moved out due to any problems with her, they were on good terms; just rearranging their living arrangements temporarily. Something to do with the fraternity needing a house-sitter for the summer, I think."

"Anyone else questioned? Besides the owner, I mean."

"Yeah. Amos said that they talked to a professor at SUNY, uh, Randall something or other, some phony sounding name...Lance Randall. The boyfriend wouldn't say much about it, but did tell the police that Amy had some sort of problem with him a couple of weeks ago, a big conflict over her final grade in his chemistry class. Amos wasn't sure of all the details, but whatever it was, maybe the old 'lay for an A' harassment, who knows, nothing formal came of it, no charges were filed. They questioned the guy only briefly. Amos says he's been in trouble like this before, but he couldn't get the go ahead to take it any farther."

"Trouble like what, the classroom thing? Or the fire?"

LaFleur looked momentarily nonplussed. "You know, that's a good question. I don't know."

"And Amos wanted to pursue it, in spite of supposedly no evidence of arson?"

"Yeah, that's what he said."

"I don't know, A.C., it sounds like there could be more to this. After what Charlie said, and now Amos tells you he has suspicions he wasn't allowed to follow up on..."

"Now, I don't know that he was all that serious, he gets overzealous sometimes."

"But if the insurance investigator hasn't even been in there yet...I still think Charlie might be right, they seem to be trying to wrap this up pretty quickly."

"Oh, hell, maybe you're right." He looked around and caught Nikki's eye as she dropped off an order at the bar,

32

and waved her over to the table. "Let's get something to eat."

As Nikki leaned over the table, Michael stammered so much giving her his order that he had to repeat it twice.

CHAPTER 5

Newton, a sleek, young tabby cat, sprawled like a washrag on the desk next to the computer monitor and watched LaFleur grow increasingly agitated. To LaFleur's own, and everyone else's surprise, he had rescued the cat in Florida and brought it home with him. He had been left behind by the previous tenants of the rental cottage, intentionally as far as anyone could determine—they had left unannounced a couple of weeks before LaFleur took the place. No one in the neighborhood knew the cat's name, or where his humans had gone. LaFleur had come in from picking lemons in the back yard one afternoon to find the cat perched on top of Westfall's biography of Isaac Newton, *Never at Rest*. LaFleur soon learned that he was a very active cat indeed, and the names suggested by the biography was just too appropriate to ignore. He had tried out "Isaac" for a few days, but the cat seemed to be annoyed by it. The name "Newton," however, worked like a charm; he even came when called, indicating to LaFleur that Newton was as clever as his namesake.

LaFleur came back after lunch with one of those nagging feelings that won't go away, like an old pop tune. This time it was the hopeless note in Maggie's sigh as she sat in the booth the other night, looking out over the river. The feeling that Maggie wasn't going to be satisfied with what little information Amos had provided was rolling around with that tune as well. So he'd called Amos back after lunch and pressed him harder on some of the details. He got the impression that Amos was not particularly happy with how the investigation was being handled, even if he wouldn't come right out and say so.

He also called Charlie Case and pumped him for more information. Charlie not only repeated what he'd said earlier, but was willing to go into more detail than when they had been in a group; he was even more adamant about his belief that there was another official Oswego whitewash in progress. This was based on information he got from a firefighter, one of the first responders, information that contradicted what the OFD arson investigator had said in public about the cause of the fire. Charlie also told LaFleur that the current investigator was given the title as a political favor over twenty years ago, and had never even been certified. Like a lot of old-school arson investigators, he worked on not much more than hunches and fire folklore.

LaFleur spent the rest of the afternoon trolling the net for whatever he could find on the Oswego fires of the last ten years. Along the way he came across several arson certification sites, which confirmed something else Charlie had mentioned, that every state has a completely different set of standards and procedures. He also came across several medical sites that described the type and treatment of serious burns. He came away with an increased appreciation of what Maggie and the doctors at the burn center—not to mention Amy—were going through.

"No, damn it all, I don't want to 'Send an error report,'" LaFleur said angrily to his computer screen. "I just want it to bloody work." He closed the offending dialog box and sat back, muttering, staring glumly at the computer screen. This was the third crash in as many minutes. He decided it was time to call in technical help. He reached for the phone and speed-dialed his new friend "Blueray," as Newton's tail twitched in sympathy.

Raymond Levy—Blueray to his friends—was one of those kids who was extremely bright but lacked focus, in LaFleur's opinion. Just out of high school, he was caught shoplifting at the local comic book store—it had been a four-dollar copy of *Howard the Duck*, nothing special—but rather than call the police right away, the comic shop owner, Arlene, an old friend of LaFleur's, called him instead. She knew LaFleur had become involved in a community youth program right before he retired, and thought Blueray could probably do better with him than with the local police. The department had become particularly unimaginative when it came to petty juvenile crimes, the result of a new task force with a particularly misguided approach to reducing overall crime stats. LaFleur learned from Arlene that things were not going well for Blueray at home at the moment, so he agreed to take him on for the summer as a personal project, give him some odd jobs to make a little money.

Like a lot of kids his age, Blueray was a self-taught computer wizard, in his case exceptionally so. LaFleur had been trying to convince Michael that Blueray would be the perfect candidate to help with digitizing medical records and keeping up the hospital's new IT installation; Michael was looking into it. He was also trying to get Blueray to look into college funding options; if anyone "deserved" to go to college, LaFleur thought he was a natural. In the meantime, LaFleur kept him busy troubleshooting his new computer.

"Yeah, hi, kid, me," LaFleur said when Blueray answered. "Got a minute?" He explained the problem, trying to provide details that he had apparently not paid enough attention to, as Blueray interrogated him without success. "Yeah. Yeah, whenever I try to open a new tab, it just hangs and then crashes. Get that damned error message. Yeah, that one." LaFleur pulled up a browser and started looking for the options menu Blueray was describing.

"Damn, I don't know," he replied to another complicated request for arcane browser configuration information. "No, I don't want to put you on speaker. Yeah, come on over, that'd be great. See you in a few."

He put the phone down and sighed. "Technology is wonderful, when it works," he said to Newton. Newton agreed, yawning as he reached out to take a casual swipe at the mouse. Windows started opening all over the desktop.

Blueray knocked once and came in, jumping from the top step down into the salon. He was tall and good-looking, starting to fill out his late-teen angular build, with an unruly mop of curly dark hair. When LaFleur first met him he had been immediately reminded of Josh Groban.

"So, what have you broken now?" Blueray said cheerfully as he walked over to the desk. LaFleur glanced bayonets at him.

"Move over, Pops, let a geek take over."

LaFleur got up as Blueray slid into the chair almost before LaFleur was out of it, then pulled a dining chair over next to him and sat down, loudly. "Yeah, well, call me a Luddite," LaFleur said grumpily, "but I don't understand the first thing about this stuff." This was obviously a ruse; Blueray knew that LaFleur almost always knew more than he let on, for any subject.

Blueray bent over the keyboard, head up and staring at the screen as admin functions popped up on the screen. "When's the last time you cleared your cache?" he asked.

"That's kind of a personal question, don't you think?"

Blueray grinned. "Or defragged your hard..."

"Very funny," LaFleur interrupted.

Blueray opened up an admin window. "What have you changed recently?" Blueray asked, fully expecting the answer that LaFleur predictably provided.

"Nothing."

Blueray just flashed him a tech-wizard grin. "Like, I believe you." There was a ghost of a question mark hanging in midair at the end of his sentence, a specter of incredulity.

"Ok, I installed some sort of plug-in the other day," LaFleur hedged, "but that should—"

"Should???" Blueray exclaimed loudly, hands over his ears, eyes wide.

They both started laughing at this. One of LaFleur's favorite ploys was to question the use of the word "should" in every context in which he heard it used. He hadn't spent over forty years as a cop, thirty of those years as a detective, without at least learning that "should" was one of the most unreliable words in the English language.

Blueray turned back to the computer. "Ok, hang on a minute. I think I know what's going on...this version is about a year old, by the way. Here, watch what I'm doing so I don't have to keep running back over here every ten minutes."

LaFleur knew how to do some of what Blueray proceeded to do, but like most computer users of his generation, didn't enjoy all the housecleaning required to keep a system up and running efficiently, and so blissfully neglected to do it. He watched as Blueray launched another system task, changed an option, then finished by rebooting the system.

As the computer crawled back to a semblance of electronic life, LaFleur went to the kitchen to get a couple of sodas. "What do you know about 'chat rooms,'" he asked on his way back in.

"What's to know? Bunch of losers sitting around lying to one another about how great they are," Blueray said derisively.

"I thought you would be a 'chat room' kind of guy," said LaFleur.

"You trying to pick a fight?" This was said with some seriousness. LaFleur detected the edginess in Blueray's voice.

"Whoa, hold on. Chat rooms aren't 'cool' anymore?"

"Not unless you're twelve years old, or some sort of pervert. You ever visit a chat room?"

"Well, not exactly." LaFleur had always thought the same way, but also assumed it was just a sign of his increasingly "senior" point of view. He was glad to get some confirmation from the younger generation that it wasn't just him. "So how would I find one?"

"Depends on what you're interested in."

"Fire," said LaFleur, handing a bottle of soda to Blueray. "I'm interested in fire."

***

There are chat rooms and then there are chat rooms, LaFleur discovered over the next two hours. He and Blueray were both surprised to find a large web presence of pyromaniacs, or professed pyros, some of whom appeared to be more or less harmless lunatics, others not so clearly harmless. The freedom of the net was something LaFleur certainly believed in, on an intellectual level, but he was having a hard time reconciling some of what they found lurking in the nether regions of cyberspace with his innate belief in the First Amendment.

Blueray knew how to use something he called an "anonymizer" to access some of the dicier sites (who knew?) in order to protect the computer's IP address from being hacked, after setting up even tighter firewall protections than he already had configured. He showed LaFleur how to set up a dummy account on the chat server. It didn't take long for them to locate a fire-themed chat room. Looking at the archives, LaFleur hesitated to characterize it as a pyromaniac site, as there were what appeared to be some legitimate discussion topics listed. But the user names they could see were unusual: "Flamer," "Vesuvius," "Lucifina"—and so on.

By some stroke of luck (LaFleur always said that the jury was still out on coincidence) a chat was active at the moment; the conversation was obviously juvenile. They watched it unfold with increasing interest; it was trivial stuff, mostly, but gradually exhibited more serious undertones. A fascination with watching campfires segued into a description of the "awesome" pictures of trees exploding in a YouTube video of a California wild fire; hilarity over some stray fireworks that set a HarborFest food tent on fire one year; plans (or had they already done this?) to set a Bridge Street bus stop shelter on fire. Then, ominously, they turned to the relative benefits and drawbacks of various fire accelerants.

"Who are these nuts, anyway?" LaFleur asked rhetorically—and was blown away when Blueray proceeded to identify at least two of the participants— "Screwy Louie" and "Flintlock"—as locals. He recognized their aliases from an online gaming site.

"These guys are really stupid," Blueray said, "using the same user names everywhere. Just a couple of stupid kids. Could even be using unsecure wi-fi. If I knew where they were sitting, I could show you every keystroke." This was probably a slight exaggeration, LaFleur thought. *He hoped.*

"My God, is this stuff really that easy to crack?" He paused. "My computer can't be hacked, can it, not with all the firewall stuff you've set up?"

Blueray laughed. "If Google can get hacked, A.C., so can you. Fortunately, no one's all that interested in you." He began jabbering away in techspeak while opening up multiple windows full of what looked like total gibberish to LaFleur. "And look at this," he pointed with his head while his fingers kept hammering the keyboard. "They aren't even trying to cover their tracks. Probably never occurred to them that Internet traffic is almost as easy to monitor as a cell phone. Amateurs." He highlighted a string of numbers in a list being displayed in a small window. "See this domain I.P. address? The one calling himself "Fudd"—he's logged in from SUNY."

CHAPTER 6

The band at Patz that night was LaFleur's favorite local group—his dentist on guitar, the mechanic from the boat shop on bass, and the local high school music teacher on sax and trombone. They were midway into *Sweet Georgia Brown*, really swinging it. LaFleur and Maggie were in his favorite Friday night spot, close to the band, in the "fish booth"— above them were three ceramic wall hangings, stylized fish with human faces. Maggie said the big one in the middle reminded her of LaFleur, something he couldn't deny. It was a very good looking fish.

It had been a long week for Maggie and she had asked LaFleur if she could stay over the weekend. The doctors and staff at the burn unit were doing their best, but were struggling to even keep Amy hydrated, she explained. The girl had still not regained consciousness.

Nikki walked up and dropped off refills—a Famous Grouse for LaFleur, vodka tonic for Maggie. LaFleur ordered a bottle of wine at the same time. After some old-school bantering with Nikki on LaFleur's part, followed by consolatory remarks from Maggie, Nikki left, laughing. Maggie sagged against LaFleur's shoulder as the band announced their break.

"Oh, to be young and foolish," she sighed.

"I'll give you foolish, but not young," LaFleur said.

"Ha." She poked him in the ribs. "What's going on between her and Michael?"

"Nikki and Michael?" he answered, his question sounding foolish even as he said it.

"You can't tell me you haven't noticed."

"Noticed what?" This earned another sharp poke. "Ouch."

"Come on, you've said it yourself. She hangs all over him. I've seen it every time I've been in here with him, anyway. And he doesn't seem to mind that much. I'm sure it's not just when I'm here. He comes in here a lot, doesn't he?"

"Well, I guess, now that you mention it—" He squirmed as she faked to her right. "Okay. So I've noticed."

"And…?" she prompted.

"What? You think they'd make a nice couple?"

This brought on a pensive look that could have been misread as a scowl. "Maybe I shouldn't have said anything. Not my business."

LaFleur sensed the sudden shift in attitude. "What?"

"Oh, nothing." She sat up. "I'm hungry," she said brightly, as Nikki approached with their dinner.

The conversation turned to life in Syracuse, from there to how Oswegonians were looked down on as being lakeside hicks. Never mind that the rest of New York looked on Syracuse as back of the beyond; only Albany had a worse reputation, and that was only because it was the center of state government. This led to local politics—always an entertaining, if simultaneously depressing—topic. After circling back to the issue of whether or not there was a cover up going on with the recent fire, LaFleur admitted that he was not so sure now that it wasn't being "swept under the rug," to use Maggie's phrase.

"I'll ask around," he promised, "see what else I can find out."

When they got home to the houseboat the subject didn't come up for the rest of the night. They were content to just lie together in bed listening to the comforting mutter and slap of water against the hull, drifting in and out of sleep until the sun through a porthole woke them up, Newton curled up between them.

CHAPTER 7

"Take a look at these," Charlie said, handing a small stack of photos to LaFleur. "From the fires," Charlie explained. They were taking a break in the game; Michael and Padre were in the galley making sandwiches. They were four-handed again, so there had been more talk than serious poker.

LaFleur went through the pictures one at a time, glancing over at Charlie to ask, "What am I looking for?"

"There are two sets of pictures there," Charlie elaborated. "One from the '98 fire, and one from the fire last week. Thought maybe you might see something in common between the two, maybe recognize somebody you'd had dealings with in the past. Arsonists are always supposed to be standing around watching as the place burns, right?"

"I suppose so. But why would I recognize anybody like that?"

"Hell, you've seen enough creeps in your day, one of them could have been mixed up in it."

"We don't even know that 'it' was arson. You said no one was ever prosecuted for the '98 fire. Or for any of the other fires, for that matter."

"That doesn't mean it wasn't arson."

Holding one of the pictures up closer, looking through his bifocals, LaFleur could just make out a few faces in a small crowd standing across the street from the pizza parlor; smoke was billowing out of the back of the building, but most of the view was blocked by a pumper. He held up another picture, this one had a clearer view of the bystanders, and a good view of the firemen attacking the blaze from the front of the storefront.

Charlie reached out and tapped the photo with his forefinger. "There, that's me on the inch and a half," he said, pointing out a fireman kneeling on the sidewalk manning a hose, pouring water onto the building. He shrugged at LaFleur's questioning look. "My wife keeps an album."

"Well, I don't know what I can do with these," LaFleur said, handing the stack back to Charlie.

"No, keep them," Charlie insisted, handing them back. "Take a closer look at them later."

"Well, alright," he said grudgingly, getting up to set the pictures over on his desk. "You ever run across any kids setting fires?" he asked over his shoulder. "You know, small stuff, but still dangerous. Fences, bus stops, old chicken coops, stuff like that?"

"Yeah, you get that once in awhile. Hardly ever catch anyone. Usually no one around by the time we get the call and get to it. Why?"

"Oh, just some stuff Blueray found on the Internet today. Wondered how common it was."

"Common enough. But usually nothing too serious."

"What about..." LaFleur started to ask, as a plate of ham and cheese on rye and four bottles of Saranac appeared from the galley with Michael and Padre. "Well, thanks for the pictures, anyway," he said, reaching for a beer.

***

Later that night, after coming across the pictures sitting on the desk again, LaFleur started thinking back over some of what he had learned earlier that day. Thinking about fire as a weapon. But not in the same sense as a gun, or a knife, or a club. Fire was far a more subtle weapon, and therefore more sinister. It allowed a murderer to remain disassociated from the crime, almost as if the death were an accident— exactly the goal, in fact, planning the fire in such a way as to make it look like an accident, destroy the evidence, and kill from a cold remove.

In spite of advances in arson investigation in the past several years, LaFleur read, there were still more suspicious fires that remained unsolved than he would have thought. Not that it was something he had given a lot of thought to in the past. Now this thing with Maggie, her involvement with the girl, the things he and Blueray had turned up that day, without even trying that hard, had made him uneasy. He jumped when the phone rang. It was Maggie. LaFleur could hardly understand her through the tears.

Amy had just died.

CHAPTER 8

St. Mary's, one of six Catholic churches in town, sits just below the hospital, on 7th Street. It is distinguished by a formidable, truly medieval looking stone bell tower with framed arch windows, few embellishments, and a tall black spire.

LaFleur slipped in through the side door, as Tommy had instructed. The serenity of an empty church was something that LaFleur appreciated much more than a service or Mass; in the soft echoes of his footsteps he heard a promise of something more to come, something he dimly envisioned as being as quiet and peaceful as the deserted pews. He agreed with Mark Twain—if he ever did get to heaven, he wouldn't want it to be an everlasting bedlam of harps, halleluiahs, and out-of-key choirs. It was as close to theology as he ever came, but it satisfied him.

Near the back of the church, Tommy had told him, was the entrance to the sacristy, and through there the door to the base of the tower. Tommy had assured him that it was okay to go through the sacristy, as it was not a sanctified area. As LaFleur made his way into the room, it was hard to suppress half-remembered altar boy duties, and the feeling of dread he had always felt when his turn came. It was a large room, by sacristy standards—plenty of room for the cabinets holding the various tools of the trade. Vestments were hanging over one credenza-like cabinet, ready for the next service. A basin stood at one end, where LaFleur knew certain items were washed, but he also noted the small lavatory off to one side, a modern convenience that Tommy had requested several years back. A small table sat in the middle of the room, cluttered with sacramental paraphernalia. A wastebasket stuffed with last week's alter flowers stood under the table at one end. No Father Tommy.

LaFleur spotted another door near the corner. That must be the way to the bell tower.

"Padre?" he called hesitantly, sticking his head through the doorway. Continuing into the tower room, LaFleur immediately saw a huge wooden stairway crawling its way up to the top of the tower. Starting on the outside wall, it ran at a forty-five degree angle up to a level platform precariously perched on several unevenly spaced square posts. The platform ended at the opposite corner. Another diagonal stairway, steeper than the first—more like a ladder than a stairway— reached from there to a trap door in the belfry itself. Worn and water-stained, the stairway had obviously seen better days. The stone walls themselves, however, were more impressive from the inside.

"Hello?" he called out again. "Father, are you up there?" He looked up towards the top of the stairway.

"Up here," he suddenly heard, a voice echoing from somewhere above and behind him. He turned in surprise.

Tommy, casually dressed in tan Bermudas and a black shirt, was hanging off the wall by a rope about forty feet off the floor. A nylon sling looped across his shoulder partially obscured his clerical collar. Silver, red, and cobalt blue carabiners and quickdraws (short slings with carabiners attached) dangled around his waist from his climbing harness like a short hula skirt. The stone wall around him was studded with bolts, hangers, and artificial hand and foot holds.

"Jumping Jesus, Padre, what are you doing up there?" LaFleur called out.

"Rock climbing in Yosemite, what does it look like?" Tommy hollered down over his shoulder. He adjusted his position so he could look down at LaFleur without twisting over backwards.

"At the moment, I'm on El Capitan, a few hundred feet off the ground," Tommy called down. "I'm already quite a few pitches up, on The Nose. Long way to go."

LaFleur just stood and stared while Tommy rappelled down in several quick hops. In a few seconds he was standing by LaFleur.

"Good climbers can make it to the top in four days," he said, "spending two nights on the wall on the way up. Of course, there are extremists who climb at night with headlamps...but they're insane, mostly."

"Insane. That's the word I was thinking of, alright. You're going to sleep while hanging off the side of a damn cliff, and you call those guys insane?"

Tommy laughed. "There are bivouac sites on the way up. Of course, if you don't make it to a site in time, you do have to sleep hanging on the wall. Some places, if there are no ledges to sleep on, you can use an artificial ledge—a 'portaledge.' I can't say I've actually ever done that. But I don't know why it would be that much different than sleeping in a small tent on the ground. As long as the wind wasn't blowing too bad." He reflected on this. "You'd have to anchor yourself in pretty tightly. Hey, maybe I can try that in here. Just to see what it's like."

"Sounds peachy."

"I'm planning to do some practice climbs in the Adirondacks later this summer," he said, coiling up the rope. "Try some simple one-pitch routes at the Beer Walls or Spider's Web, later maybe tackle something at Poke-O at Lake Champlain. Nothing too daunting—I'm not as strong and agile as I used to be, but even at my age I should be able to handle the easier routes." He looked over at LaFleur. "I'll need a partner, a belayer," he said. "Interested?"

"Belay that," LaFleur snorted.

Tommy laughed and looped the rope over a hook near the stairway.

In the meantime LaFleur had noticed that there were rings—hangers, Tommy called them—bolted to every wall, some up to a formidable height, and what looked like maps or pictures attached to the wall at various points. "What is all this?" he asked, waving his hand around over his head. "Are those maps?"

"Yes, exactly. I've built my own practice walls," answered Tommy, "complete with documentation. Maps, photos, instructions on how various pitches are typically ascended, posted at key positions on the routes. All the

51

best: El Cap, in Yosemite, that's the one I was just on; Eiger, over on the west wall, you know that one; and back over there," leaning back and raising an arm, "are two popular routes in the Frankenjura area, in Germany; a parishioner recommended those, I had never heard of them."

"And you say you are in training for all of these? To really climb them?"

"Well, I can't say I'm actually 'training' for these specific sites—there are way too many routes, and real routes are nowhere near as simple as this wall. But it keeps me in shape, if nothing else. The pictures and maps are just for fun. Something to inspire me. Someday, though, I'd sure like to give one of the big ones a try."

"You said you wanted to talk about something." Tommy said as he led LaFleur back into the sacristy. "What's on your mind?" he pulled a couple of chairs over to the table.

"You mentioned the other day that you knew the family who lost a son in that fire a few years ago," LaFleur said as they sat down. "That you had counseled them?" Tommy nodded, not sure where this was going. "Did they ever say anything to you about being satisfied—or dissatisfied, rather—with the investigation that was done?"

The Father looked down at the floor before answering. "And if they had?" he asked.

"It could have a bearing on the investigation being done—not being done, according to Charlie, and Maggie—on the recent fire," said LaFleur. "Maggie is convinced that not enough attention is being given to certain aspects of that fire; Charlie has said much the same thing. And now that the girl has died, and still nothing, yet…"

"Did you know that I am also counseling Amy's parents? And her boyfriend Robbie, too."

"No." He waited for Tommy to continue. It was a long time before Tommy spoke again, and when he did, it was not what LaFleur wanted to hear.

"You recall what you told Maggie last year, after everything fell apart in your investigation into Angie's death? With no chance left of proving that either one of your suspects was guilty of murder, or even involved in some sort of cover-up? You told her that 'justice is where you find it.' Yes, she and I talked quite a bit after you left for Florida," he said to LaFleur's raised eyebrows. "Justice, forgiveness. Should be two sides of the same coin, A.C., but seldom found in the same place at the same time. And do you remember what *I* told *you*? About justice?"

"You said that even though justice was God's, a little earthly justice now and then never hurt anything," LaFleur answered quietly.

"Yes." Tommy said. "Yes."

CHAPTER 9

Steamer's Bar was busy, as usual on a Friday afternoon. Nikki sat at a table against the wall, nursing a beer and listening to the conversations swirling around her. She seldom went out, but didn't feel like going home just yet.

The waitress came by with a menu. Nikki didn't know her, she looked like a college student. Nikki paged through the menu idly; she wasn't that hungry, but knew she'd better eat something, not just sit there and drink all evening.

The woman at the table directly across from her was drinking white wine. Nikki thought that women drinking white wine looked…prissy. Trying to show how sophisticated they were. *Oh, I guess I'll have the Chardonnay—that's not too oaky, is it? Hmm, well, maybe a Pinot Grigio, then, thanks so much.* Nikki stared at her while taking a large swig of beer. The woman kept glancing over at her, sensing that she was being watched. Nikki took another large gulp of beer and looked away.

She watched as a waitress took orders at a nearby table, suddenly dreading the thought of giving the waitress her order. You'd think, she said to herself, that after waiting on other people all day I would enjoy being waited on for a change. Then why do I feel like I am taking advantage of someone? I don't mind waitressing, why should I think another waitress would mind waiting on me? She tried to remember her junior college psychology: transference? identity crisis? Well, she hadn't liked psychology all that much.

Was she being too pushy with Dr. Fuentes—Michael? He was always with LaFleur, which was becoming very annoying. She didn't trust LaFleur. She knew about the incident at the hospital last year, some of it, at least; LaFleur's friend, Maggie, he'd almost gotten her killed, and Michael saved her. She didn't really know much more than that.

Was Michael stringing her along? He didn't have any other girlfriends, she knew at least that much. She really did like Michael a lot, she decided. This was going to be hard. But she was confident that she could work it out. She planned to get what she needed in the end.

She picked up the People magazine she'd brought with her—someone had left it earlier that day in a booth at Patz—and read the cover headlines. A caption under a picture of a two big Hollywood stars read "Chemistry on the Movie Set." Why was it always "chemistry" between movie stars?

She remembered some college chemistry; before she was forced to drop out, it had been her favorite course. She'd never liked the term "chemistry" applied to relationships—it was too volatile. In a chemical reaction, something was always changed. There had been one experiment in particular that had fascinated her: weigh a small piece of filter paper on an extremely sensitive scale, then burn it, very carefully saving the ash; then weigh the ash and determine how much of the paper was lost through combustion.

Just like relationships. They could burn fast and hot, but when the affair was over, something was always lost.

CHAPTER 10

Diethyl ether, though sometimes used as an accelerant in arson fires, is not typically an arsonist's first choice. The old standbys of kerosene, turpentine, charcoal lighter fluid, gasoline—these were what the average fire investigator expected to find traces of at any fire scene suspected of being arson, not something as volatile and hard to handle as ether. Ether was also not something you could buy at the corner hardware store or gas station.

LaFleur's sudden interest in ether as an arson accelerant was prompted by a visit from Charlie Case, who had stopped by with an update on the recent fire. He was as dismissive of the skills of the department fire investigator as ever, and never expected that an in-depth investigation would be carried out; he was surprised to learn that there had in fact been some accelerant testing done.

Charlie's informant in the department told him that no traces of the standard accelerants were found, but that ether had been put forward as a possibility; something about the discovery of a peroxide residue that was fairly easy to test for with not much more than a drop of potassium iodide on a paper test strip. Charlie conceded that as no elaborate testing was required, it might just be true. He also knew that an arson investigator from the insurance company was supposed to verify any preliminary findings. Apparently they were not completely satisfied with the report provided by the OFD.

The internet crash course in chemistry that LaFleur put himself through that afternoon left him with a new set of nagging questions. How hard was it to get hold of ether? Would Michael know? It wasn't used much anymore as an anesthetic, if at all, if he remembered correctly. Would there be any at the hospital? Can it be easily purchased from a chemical supply house?

He had also been struggling through various papers on the web, on gas chromatography, isotope mass spectrometry, and other equally arcane subjects. He learned just enough to make him suspicious of how much he was actually understanding.

He looked up as Newton leaped up to the top of the bookcase behind him; he was still not quite accustomed to how much noise a single cat could make, even just moving around. Something suddenly fell onto the desk next to him as Newton rummaged around up there. It was a SUNY directory LaFleur had forgotten about; he couldn't even remember where he got it or why he still had it.

He picked it up and started to throw it back up onto the top of the bookcase—Newton had jumped back down already, mission accomplished—then changed his mind and instead started to pitch it into the recycle box in the corner. Then he had another thought.

Maybe he would give that chemistry professor a call.

CHAPTER 11

They didn't know exactly what they were looking for, as is often the case, but they knew it when they found it.

The desk was littered with photos—cut outs from newspapers, prints off of the internet, snapshots from Charlie's wife, a set of glossies from a local photographer that Michael had talked to the week before—all dating from 1998 to the present. They were slowly sorting them by date and location. Newton sprawled over a stack of discards at one end of the desk.

Whenever LaFleur found something particularly interesting among the hardcopies, he passed it to Michael, sitting next to him at a portable table, to scan. The scanner was on loan from Blueray, who had brought it over earlier that day. At the same time he had loaded some sophisticated image comparison software onto LaFleur's computer.

LaFleur was getting impatient. They had been going over the photos for almost two hours, Michael scanning, LaFleur laboriously making notes in a small notebook, classifying each photo. Based on what they had heard from Charlie Case, and assuming that this had not yet been done by either the fire department or the police, they were trying to identify anyone appearing in the photos from the various fires; more specifically, anyone appearing at more than one of the fires. So far they were not having a lot of luck, even with the imaging program. They were able to determine only two faces in common. One, a man, appeared across the street from both pizza parlor fires, LaFleur recognized as a local business man, the owner of the bookstore on the opposite corner from the second fire. The store was also only about two blocks from the site of the earlier fire, so it was not surprising that he should appear at both fires.

The other figure, a woman, was flagged by the imaging program as being common to three of the photos, but the face was too indistinct to make out her features clearly. What was interesting, though, was the fact that the face was picked out of photos of three different fires, all at Pi Rho Delta fraternity houses—one in Buffalo in 2001, another in Rochester in 2004, and the one in Oswego, just a few weeks ago. All three fires were unexplained—the latest had been provisionally blamed on smoking, a cigar left burning in a TV lounge—but the frat boys had denied it, and Charlie Case had his doubts. There was another reference to a fraternity fire in Oswego from the mid-seventies, but they discounted that as out of their range of interest. They put in a call to Blueray to see if he'd come over the next day and help them clean up the images.

They'd promised themselves they wouldn't start drinking until after four P.M. It was 4:04 when LaFleur pushed his chair back and stood and walked to the galley, calling over his shoulder as he went, "Want a beer?" He already had a couple of Saranacs out of the fridge before Michael had a chance to answer.

"So, what do you think? Are we wasting our time here?" LaFleur asked.

Michael reached over and took the Saranac that LaFleur was holding out to him. "No, not at all. We've made a lot of progress. We know how the image software works now; we've almost got everything scanned; from here on it's just a matter of plowing through it all. A challenge, but kind of a nice change of pace." He stood and stretched. "Let's take a closer look at what I've been scanning," he said.

LaFleur went back to the desk and sat down. Michael stood looking over his shoulder, watching as LaFleur opened up photos from the two local fires, panning and zooming over groups of spectators.

"Oops, zoomed right past that guy," he said, and backed out a bit. "Does he look familiar?"

"Not really."

Drumming his fingers lightly on the keyboard, LaFleur kept staring at the face for a few seconds.

"Ah. It's that crackpot, weird name…supposedly tried to set some fraternity house on fire years and years ago? Big deal for awhile in the "Letters to the Editor" section of the *Palladium Times*, as I recall." He drummed a little more, starting to tap out the rhythm to *Bumble Boogie*. "Elihu Reen."

"Huh?"

"That's the old guy's name, Elihu Reen. Coming back to me. He used to own a bar downtown, a real dive, the

'Port City' something or other. No, the 'Lighthouse Bar,' that was it. We were in there off and on, used to issue a lot of underage violations. Guess I need to talk to Amos about this guy; I'd completely forgotten about him, somehow. While the newspapers played up the alleged arson thing, he even picked up a nickname: "Matchstick."

"Why 'Matchstick?'"

"Well, he's skinny as a rail. I think at the time of the newspaper article some fraternity student found out he used to work at the old Diamond Match plant in town. It was a stretch, but the name stuck. They plastered posters all over the neighborhood, accusing him of the arson and the police of failing to arrest him." He made a note to follow up on Reen, but at the same time told Michael, "I doubt that we'll get anywhere with Reen. I think he's just an old eccentric that the frat boys found to be an easy target."

He started panning around the buildings involved in the fire again, when Michael leaned forward and pointed to the screen.

"What's that?"

LaFleur zoomed in to the point Michael was indicating. "Looks like graffiti. Not too unusual in that neighborhood." The image started to shrink.

"Wait a second. It doesn't look like your average tag. Go back."

"Okay." This time LaFleur zoomed in on the exact spot until it became blurry from high magnification. "Not enough resolution."

"Try enhancing it."

"Just like the spy movies, huh?" He opened a couple of menus, looking for the right option.

"Here it is." He drew a selection box around the figures and clicked Sharpen. "That's a little better. Still doesn't look like much."

"Hit it again."

LaFleur opened a dialog and used a slider to raise the effect to a higher level.

"That's Greek," said Michael, as the figures came into better focus.

"Isn't that one character a mathematical symbol? It looks like 'pi.' You know, 3.1415 and whatever."

"Yeah, that's 'pi.' The other character is 'rho.'"

"So, what've we got here? 'Rho' and 'pi.'"

Michael didn't answer for a moment.

"No, what we've got here is 'pi' and 'rho.'" He took a pull from his Saranac.

They looked at one another.

"Sonofabitch."

They kept going over the photos until they were bleary-eyed; the enhancement software didn't work nearly as well as it always did in the movies, even though Blueray called with some pointers. The Greek symbols intrigued and frustrated them, and research led to several pyromania web sites, some legitimate, some suspect. LaFleur was nervous about visiting a couple of the sites, but trusted Blueray's protective measures to do their job. Speculations on the Oswego fires ran rampant, from reasonable explanations for nearly everything they had uncovered to grand conspiracy theories involving local and state government. About the only thing left out was UFOs.

The rash of fires in Oswego—that couldn't be typical, could it? Were other small towns plagued with similar runs of unfortunate events, fires or otherwise? They googled for statistics on Syracuse, Rochester, even some of the smaller towns like Auburn or Utica; nothing jumped out.

Dinner was a bucket of spaghetti from Canale's, along with Maggie's last bottle of Eye of the Swan. Suddenly it was very late; by a strange coincidence, the bottle of Famous Grouse sitting in the center of the table was almost empty.

"I'm behind on my recycling this week," LaFleur said. "I need this empty bottle to make my quota." He poured the last of the scotch into his and Michael's glasses. "You can stay over," he added to Michael as an afterthought.

"Damn good idea." Michael raised his glass. He'd just come off of ten straight days of on-call, and needed some R&R.

While talking about the various class divisions that seemed prevalent in Oswego—being both a blue-collar and a university town, there was a long-standing tension in the community between "towns" and "gowns," had been for as long as LaFleur could remember. LaFleur had been reminded of the conversation he'd had with Michael previously, joking about Nikki being "out of his class," and Michael's uncomfortable reaction. What could be going on there?

"Speaking of townies," LaFleur said, even though that had been at least an hour ago, "what do you have against Nikki Faghin? I know you well enough, I hope, to know that it's not really a townie thing, am I right?"

"Now, A.C., I really don't—"

"Now, I'm not trying to pry—well, no, I guess I am. You don't seem to have much of a social life, Michael, if I can be blunt about it. Or at least you never talk about it. And Nikki—she's pretty, seems fairly bright and personable, has a crush on you a mile wide; am I missing something here? You're not, are you, well...you know..."

The sigh Michael let go had the sound of not just frustration, but almost anguish. "A.C., if I could..." He trailed off.

"Could what?" LaFleur wasn't in the mood to let it drop for some reason; and after all, he was trying to be sympathetic.

After a smaller sigh, followed by a look of supreme resignation, Michael drained his glass. "Got any more of this stuff?"

While LaFleur went to the galley to get another bottle and some fresh ice, Michael began talking, hesitating, starting and stopping, almost talking to himself. He waited for LaFleur to sit back down at the table before starting again.

"So. It's not about Nikki," he said. "I *like* Nikki. But I am just not able to start any kind of romantic relationship with her—with anybody, really. It's....it's complicated."

"Well, if you don't—""

"No, you've got me started now, let me finish. I should have told you this a long time ago, I suppose; but no one here knows this. Maggie's the only person I've told." He took a sip of his drink. "Before I came to Oswego, I was practicing in Lexington, Kentucky. The practice I had wasn't a great one, and not something I was all that crazy about, but it was working okay. I had two partners when I set it up originally. One guy, a Pakistani, left after just a few weeks to go back to Lahore, his daughter was getting married or something, and he decided to go back home to stay for awhile. Anyway. That left me and the other anesthesiologist, a guy by the name of Larry Kulski. Dr.

Lawrence Z. Kulski. The 'Z' stood for 'Zoltan,' of all things." He paused and took a drink before continuing.

"So, we had this small practice; the two of us got along okay, but didn't see each other that much, hardly ever got together socially. Things went along like that for awhile." He looked away, shifting in his chair. "We'd had a couple of different office managers over the space of a few months, but they kept leaving, too, so we both thought it was great when Larry's wife—Shana—took over managing the office. She was a CPA, had been at Arthur Anderson before that all fell apart; she had been really good at her job, but hadn't gone back to work full time anywhere, and now she just took over everything for us; billing, taxes, all of it.

"I saw her quite a bit; I was terrible at bookkeeping, and she was very enthusiastic, very helpful. We got along great. We went out to dinner occasionally when Larry was tied up at the hospital. Nothing more at first. Then she told me that she and Larry had not been getting along, for quite a long time, apparently, and, um…well, I suppose you can guess what happened. We had an affair; very heavy, lots of sneaking around, lots of guilt, but a lot of guilty pleasure, too. This went on for awhile. Then…" Michael stopped again.

A melting ice cube tinkled in LaFleur's glass. He hesitated, then asked, "Well, I still don't see what that has to do with Nikki…?"

"Yeah, well. If that's all there had been to it," Michael replied, "I wouldn't have any trouble telling you this, and I wouldn't have any trouble dating Nikki, or anyone else, for that matter. As I would like to. Date, that is. But what happened, what makes this all so hard, is…God damn it."

Michael stood up and walked around the salon for minute, swirling his drink. He sat back down.

"He caught us. In his house. In bed. And he pulled out a gun and shot her."

LaFleur rocked back in his chair. "Jesus, Mary, and Joseph."

Michael went on, staring into his glass. "Then he shot me. Shot *at* me. Hit me in the arm." He pulled up his sleeve and exposed a large, mottled scar just above his left elbow. "Just missed the humerus. Guess he was too agitated by then to take careful aim."

He looked up at LaFleur. "A few seconds later Larry put the gun to his head and pulled the trigger. He died instantly," Michael said. "Shana died before the paramedics arrived."

With one eye partly open, Michael watched from the couch as LaFleur diced a potato, then threw it into the pan; bacon, onions, and sausage were already frying. As soon as the potatoes were browned, LaFleur poured in a bowl of scrambled eggs, stirred it up a bit, then tossed in some chopped green chiles. He saw that Michael was finally awake.

"Slumgullion, coming up," LaFleur called over his shoulder. "My old man used to make this on fishing trips. Everything you need to get you going after a hard night."

Rolling off the couch slowly so as not to disturb Newton, who was stretched out at his feet, Michael made his way into the galley. "Coffee?" he croaked.

LaFleur pointed to the cupboard next to the sink. "Cups up there, coffee's ready, over on the counter."

As they ate breakfast, LaFleur pointedly made no mention of Michael's revelations of the night before. He figured that if Michael wanted to talk about it anymore, he'd bring it up himself. Which he did, as soon as they had finished off the slumgullion.

"Thanks for listening last night, A.C. I've been wanting to talk to someone about it—other than my therapist—but there's not many people around here I could trust with something like that. Well, of course, Maggie; I told you that she's the only other person who knows about it."

"You give any more thought to my advice?"

"Asking Nikki out?" He got up and poured himself the last cup of coffee. "Yeah, I've been thinking about it, for awhile, as a matter of fact. I get the same advice from Dr. Rostrow, actually—she's the psychiatrist I've been seeing—but haven't had the courage to follow through." He sat down. "But you're right, I can't go on like this. I'll stop by and talk to Nikki."

"When?" LaFleur couldn't resist asking.

"Soon, A.C. Soon"

"But when?"

"Okay, okay. Today. Is that soon enough?"

"That'll do," LaFleur said, raising his empty cup. "Is there any more coffee?"

CHAPTER 12

LaFleur sat gazing out the window at Patz, watching the light play on the water. Michael's story from the night before was still on his mind, but the river was having its usual calming effect.

Shaking off his reverie, he set his beer down and pulled a business card from his shirt pocket and glanced at it, refreshing his memory: "*Debra Gallatin – Special Services Group, Allied Insurance,*" he read. Charlie had set him up with the arson investigator who'd just arrived in town. He checked his watch: a few minutes after four. She should be here any time now.

He looked up just as she came in. Maybe he still had a touch of old-fashioned chauvinism lurking about in his psyche; his first thought was *hot damn*. She was small and svelte, forty-something, with long, dark auburn hair—darker than Maggie's, he reflexively thought—dressed to kill in a satiny blouse and a dark, short skirt. She walked like Gisele Bündchen coming down the fashion runway, but somehow making it look natural.

She identified him as her appointment immediately, before he could even stand up, waving to him as she came through to the bar. He did manage to stand by the time she got to him.

"Detective LaFleur?"

"Yes, right. Pleased to meet you." He stuck out his hand, which she grasped warmly. He tried not to look instantly enamored, failed, though she must be used to it, he thought.

"Pleased to meet *you*," she replied. "Charlie said—"

"Ah, don't tell me. I'd just have to deny it all."

She laughed; not politely, he felt, but a nice, sincere laugh. *Good start.*

He steered her towards one of the window booths. Tried not to look at her legs as she slid into the booth.

"So," she said, "I understand you are assisting the fire department in their investigation?"

"Is that what Charlie said? I'm not."

She demurred. "Maybe I exaggerated. He did say you were not *officially* involved. But also that you were in fact doing a serious investigation. It seemed clear that he expects more out of you than he expects from the department's investigator."

"All I'm hoping to do is determine if there are things being—overlooked. As a favor to a friend."

"Ah, that would be Ms. Malone? The nurse?"

He nodded. "Charlie really filled you in."

"Yes, he sure did," she agreed. "But what exactly do you expect from me? I can't promise much, I'm afraid.

Especially not without knowing more about what it is you are after, in any case."

"I appreciate that. Not a problem; I'll tell you everything I know. And more to the point, what I don't. But I'm sure there is a lot of information that, well, things I really would like to know, but, you know, I no longer have the authority…" He sensed a slight defensive shift in her posture as he stumbled. "I would not expect you to divulge any sensitive information," he stressed. "Not unless…"

"Unless?"

"Unless it would help us both."

"I'm not sure I understand."

"Would you like something to drink?"

After the first glass of wine, Debra agreed to stay for dinner. She'd even expense it, she said. She had obviously come to trust LaFleur; he told her about the chat rooms, the rumors of traces of ether at the site, the chemistry professor's run in with the girl, Amy, and the suspicious graffiti—though she told him that true pyromaniacs were seldom also serious arsonists.

In response to his careful prying, she in turn revealed that she did indeed feel that there was a certain amount of stonewalling going on in her dealings with the police and fire departments. She did not hazard a guess as to why this would be so; he got the impression that she had seen it so often that it was no surprise. She also confirmed that evidence of diethyl ether had been found at the most recent fire scene. Even as volatile as ether was, she said, it still appeared in more arsons than might be expected.

He was surprised to hear her confirm what Charlie had hinted at, that many arson investigators not only weren't properly qualified, but that many of the techniques they used had been either discounted or totally overturned in recent years: concrete spalling, alleged "arson" burn patterns on floors and walls, flash fires, crazed or broken windows, all had been debunked as conclusive arson indicators. She described the tragic case of a man who had actually been executed in Illinois based on unwarranted conclusions given as evidence by a local investigator.

"How about insurance scams? Common?" LaFleur asked.

"No, not as common as most people imagine," she answered. "It's too easy to show financial motive. Most who try the route get found out pretty easily."

"Nothing in the latest fires to point in that direction?"

"No, nothing. And I've checked the history on a couple of older Oswego fires, the earlier pizza parlor fire, for example. That was initially thought to be owner-arson, for the insurance, but the evidence was very slim and it wasn't pursued. But based on what I could find, it's very unlikely that it was done for the insurance."

This matched what he and Michael had learned as well. So, if insurance had been ruled out as a motive, why wasn't the department investigation being expanded?

"And your investigation?" LaFleur pressed.

Swirling a last bit of wine in her glass, she hesitated before answering. "Hate to sound like a cheap movie, but, you know, 'I'm really not at liberty to say.'"

He chuckled at this. "Yeah, I know the drill. But if at some point there's something you can let go of, you know I'll appreciate it. Buy you dinner next time."

"It's a deal."

After they left the restaurant—LaFleur sauntering down to the marina, Debra walking off in the other direction down 1st Street towards the Captain's Quarters—LaFleur

73

couldn't help feeling a little guilty over having such a good time. He'd not been with a woman he liked as well—other than Maggie, of course—for many years. He thought he sensed a reciprocal feeling on her part. He wasn't sure what to think about that.

His thoughts quickly turned back to the fires. He didn't know how long Debra would be in town, and wanted to be ready to meet with her again—not that he wasn't already ready.

CHAPTER 13

The day after the long session Michael had spent at LaFleur's, Michael and Nikki had their first date; she'd accepted almost before he'd finished asking her, and even suggested they make it the same night. Since Michael was going on call later in the week, he agreed. They went to a movie, that old stand-by of dating—neutral territory—and afterwards spent the rest of the evening at Nikki's, just talking. They discovered they had more in common than either had thought.

Sitting on flimsy plastic chairs on the tiny balcony of her apartment—Nikki lived on the upper floor of a large converted Victorian boarding house overlooking the harbor—she told him what it had been like growing up as a "townie." Her mother checked at the local Price Chopper, and her father was a welder who had worked on the reactor at Nine Mile One. Nikki later worked at the same Price

Chopper while in high school, stocking shelves, after her father died. There had been some bureaucratic confusion over death benefits, or a snag in the distribution of the pension, she had never been too sure what, exactly, and they'd waited years to get their money. Once things improved, she said, she'd planned to go to college—she wanted to become a nurse—but that hadn't worked out for some reason she was reluctant to elaborate on.

Waving her wine glass around, talking about the school canteens, the football games, the nights at the bowling alley, she seemed willing, even eager, to reminisce about her high school days. She was reticent about what followed. Michael pressed lightly and was rebuffed. He got the impression that she was still something of a loner; her only friends were co-workers at Patz, and she seldom saw them outside of work. She'd given up any aspirations to go back to school, or try to do anything beyond waitressing. Once a townie always a townie, she said.

Michael empathized. He'd grown up—also fatherless— in the Dominican Republic, in one of the poorer sections of the southern city of Santo Domingo. His mother took in laundry, which in later years caused Michael to marvel at what a stereotypical "third world" upbringing he'd had. He'd started working at age eight, shining shoes in the church plaza, carrying bags at the bus station, cadging an odd job wherever he could.

His big break, the money to get him first into a private school, then into medical school, had come from another unlikely source—they both laughed at the utter improbability of it—the proverbial "rich uncle." His mother's sister had married well above her station, a local politician who went on to become influential in government in the aftermath of the Trujillo dictatorship. Once he was old enough to understand that his uncle was part of a corrupt political machine, Michael had for a time felt somewhat guilty over the source of the money—oh, but why? Nikki said—but as corruption was the rule rather than the exception, he eventually came to accept it. He now tried to pay back what he could by doing extended stints of volunteer work at hospitals back in the D.R.

They'd parted that night with a kiss—the first real kiss for either of them in a long time—and made a date for Friday.

CHAPTER 14

"Come in," LaFleur heard in answer to his knock. He pushed open the door and walked into Lance Randall's office, blinking his eyes at a mass of dust motes hanging in a brilliant shaft of light from the room's single window. As his eyes adjusted, he could see that stacks of journals, papers, and books took up every square inch of desk and shelf space, flooding out onto the floor and window sills. Randall was at a large shabby desk in the corner, bent over an open manila folder. He looked up distractedly and motioned LaFleur to the empty chair beside it. "Please. Be with you in two seconds."

LaFleur took a seat, blinking as his eyes now had to readjust to the dimmer surroundings, out of the direct sunlight. While he waited, he looked around the office. Located behind Snygg, the main science building, Randall's office in Piez Hall was apparently not one of the more prestigious on campus; no view of the lake, even if the window had been facing that direction. Several diplomas were displayed in tacky frames on the wall: Randall had done his undergraduate work at Harvey Mudd College, in California. A good school, LaFleur knew; he wondered how Randall had gotten from there to here. Both a Master's and PhD degree were also on the wall; Randall'd done his Master's at Oswego, his doctorate at SUNY, Buffalo. And yet he was still only an assistant professor? Why hadn't he gone further by now? Hanging next to the degrees was a faded fraternity certificate, but he couldn't make out any details.

After five more minutes, LaFleur picked up a two-year-old *Journal of Applied Chemistry* from the stack next to his chair and started leafing through it. This succeeded in getting Randall's attention, who had the good manners to pretend to be embarrassed.

"Sorry to keep you waiting. Grades were due yesterday."

"No problem," LaFleur answered. *Not for me, anyway.*

Randall finally closed the folder he had been working with and turned to face LaFleur. "So, Detective…?"

"LaFleur."

"Yes, thanks. Detective LaFleur, what was it you wanted again? You said something on the phone about a computer theft?"

The earlier call to make the appointment had been short. The professor had agreed to the visit more readily than LaFleur had expected, falling for a rather unlikely story, that LaFleur was following up on a report of computer hacking suspected to have originated in one of the chemistry offices. It was a fairly simple matter of misdirection, a skill LaFleur had honed over the years to a

79

fine edge. Randall had not even asked under whose authority LaFleur was working.

"Not exactly," LaFleur answered. "More like unauthorized use of school resources. So, computer theft in a way, but I'm more interested in the actual context of the online access, rather than the access itself."

"I don't quite follow you. Can you be more specific?"

"Sure. Sorry to be vague, but we're following several threads. One has to do with someone using a SUNY account to access, well, questionable sites. Something that might even lead to criminal activity, if there is a connection made to certain events."

The look on Randall's face told LaFleur that he had succeeded in exasperating the professor. That should put him off his guard a bit.

"To be specific"—*finally*, said Randall's expression—"we think there may be a connection between someone in this building logging into certain types of chat rooms—'fire bug' sites—and the recent pizza parlor fire. Apartment fire, I should say, the apartments above were damaged more than the restaurant. And this could go beyond just the restaurant fire. There's been a rash of vandalism, some of it involving small fires. Fortunately nothing too serious, as of yet. But, then again—you might know that there was a recent fire at a local fraternity house?" Randall nodded warily. "So, we're looking at a wide range of possible leads, beyond what the police have already looked at, you know, fire hazards, insurance scams. We're also looking for someone with access to university computer resources. A possible college or frat connection, what with the fraternity arson attempts. And, maybe, someone with a knowledge of chemistry."

"Now, just a minute—" Randall exclaimed, anxiously pushing his chair back from his desk.

"Some student," LaFleur quickly reassured him, "or an outside hacker, possibly, someone looking for both information and computer access."

Appearing somewhat mollified, Randall pulled himself back up to the edge of the desk, still grasping the edge tightly. "What, exactly, do you want to know?" he asked.

"A couple of things. Let's start with chemistry. What can you tell me about fire accelerants?"

"In general? I don't know anything about arson..."

"Well, more specifically, then—could dimethyl ether be used as an accelerant?"

A puzzled look preceded Randall's answer. "I suppose so, but I wouldn't think it would be a good choice."

"Why not?"

"Volatility. Evaporates quickly, fumes are highly explosive. There is a strict protocol established for dealing with ether in the lab. Any small flame, or even a slight spark, will set it off. And, by the way, when it dries it forms explosive peroxides. Difficult stuff to deal with in the open."

"Word has it that traces were found at the site of the fire. How would that be detected?"

"Iodides."

"Is that complicated?"

"Not really. Do you need details?"

"No," LaFleur demurred, "that's okay." He paused. "Could it be mixed with something? To make it easier to handle, I mean."

"Well, it's not that miscible," Randall said. "Mixes slightly with water, or oils. Or methanol, things like that. But that doesn't sound like a good way to use it as an accelerant to me. Were other chemicals detected along with the ether?"

"Not that I know of," LaFleur answered carefully. "But I want to know the right questions to ask when I get the chance. That information is helpful." He reached into his pocket and pulled out a small notebook. "Is ether easy to come by, outside of a laboratory environment?"

"I don't really know. How about hospitals?" he added helpfully.

"Good idea. I'll check into that." He already knew—as should Randall—that, one, ether was difficult to obtain outside of a laboratory or other commercial enterprise; and two, ether was no longer used in anesthesia.

"Back to my earlier question," LaFleur said. "Have you ever heard any students refer to any fire-related chat rooms or web sites, or heard of anyone called by the nicknames of 'Flintlock,' or, let's see, 'Screwy Louie?'"

Randall snorted a short laugh. "Screwy Louie? No, no I haven't. Neither one of them."

"Hmmm." He glanced absently around the room, then stopped with a sudden jolt of uneasiness as he focused on a nameplate: Lance Randal, PhD. *Phd. Phud. Fudd?* "How about 'Fudd?" he asked.

"What, like Elmer Fudd? What next, Bugs Bunny?" Randall was still snickering, apparently sincere in his ignorance of any of these names.

"Well, I had to ask. Pretty silly, I guess." LaFleur twisted in his chair, paused for the briefest moment, then continued. "You had some connection, I believe, to the girl who died in the fire?" He leaned forward.

"Amy?"

***

LaFleur sat on a bench next to Lake Ontario, behind the lot where he had parked, down across Rudolph Road. It was a permit only lot, but the campus was nearly deserted; finals were over, most students had gone home. SUNY didn't have a huge summer program.

He seldom worried about the effect of his questions on suspects, but couldn't help feeling a little remorseful over the reaction he had seen in Randall's face at his question about Amy; he'd looked genuinely distraught.

Still, staring out over the lake, LaFleur had to remind himself how many times in the past he had seen a similar reaction, in similar circumstances, and how many times that reaction had been false.

Which was this?

During the interview, he hadn't noticed any particular reaction to his queries about accelerants. Randall simply confirmed some of the basic information LaFleur already had, and had not seemed at all hesitant or suspicious about that line of questioning. The same with the internet leads; Randall didn't appear to be the type to engage in the sorts of juvenile chats that he and Blueray found. Even after LaFleur pushed him a little bit more on it later in the interview, he came across as slightly contemptuous; again LaFleur had seen no overt signs of covering up.

He stood up and started back to the car, then decided to walk over to Rudy's Lakeside café for lunch. While he walked along the shore, he thought over Randall's responses to his last questions about Amy. The quick denial, followed by the equally quick admission to having had her in a class. The evasion concerning the grading conflict, only admitted after realizing that LaFleur had details that could only have come from some sort of official report. The distress over her death. All explainable, all potentially innocent, if evasive. Randall had cut the interview short at that point, claiming grading pressure. LaFleur acquiesced, more or less satisfied with Randall's answers. But by the time he got to Rudy's he started having serious second thoughts—when it came to the professor's relationship with Amy, he was not ready to dismiss some kind of connection to the fire, however tenuous.

As he slid into a booth by a window at Rudy's, he called Maggie. He thought he should get her opinion: was he getting too far off the track? Even if there had been some kind of scholastic conflict between him and Amy, it hadn't appeared to be that serious, and despite the nagging doubt, as far as LaFleur could tell nothing else had been going on.

"Maggie? Hi. I'm at Rudy's. Just talked to the professor."

"And?" She waited expectantly.

"I still don't know."

"What do you mean?" she asked. "Don't know?"

"Well, I'm still not convinced he's involved—"

She cut him off. "Have you talked to Robbie yet?" Maggie asked.

"Amy's boyfriend? No, not yet."

"Talk to him. Then go back and talk to that professor again."

This was turning into a long day.

After he finished his lunch, he called Father Tommy to find out how he could get in touch with Amy's boyfriend. It happened that the Father was going to see Robbie that afternoon, in just a few minutes, actually. Would LaFleur like to come over and talk to him before their appointment?

On the way over, LaFleur tried to rehearse what he would say to the boy. As it turned out, Robbie was a little late, and this gave LaFleur a few extra minutes to talk things over with Tommy beforehand; otherwise he was sure he'd have blown it. It was hard enough even with Tommy's help. Robbie was struggling to maintain, but LaFleur could tell he was on the edge. The Father had enlisted the aid of a psychiatrist, a member of the congregation who offered to treat Robbie free of charge. Robbie's parents' insurance may have paid a portion of the cost of psychiatric care, but they were relieved to get help for him without the additional uncertainty of how to pay for it.

After talking with Robbie for only about ten minutes, LaFleur was convinced that Maggie had been right in insisting. Robbie had laid out a disturbing scenario, between episodes of breaking down, just trying to talk about Amy. About his guilt over not being there that night. At that point Robbie had had to leave the room for several minutes. When he came back, he brought some of Amy's grade reports and other documentation they had planned to use in the sexual harassment claim against Randall. In a shaky but determined voice, Robbie laid out exactly what Amy had been subjected to. After he finished, LaFleur was convinced that there was something very suspicious in the posturing he had just seen in Randall.

Just before he left, he thought to ask Robbie why he'd been away from the apartment.

"The Zeta house needed someone to do some maintenance and house-sit for a couple of weeks. Just a temporary thing, most everyone was away."

"So you're a member of that fraternity, the 'Zeta' fraternity?" LaFleur asked.

"Zeta Tau Alpha. No, I'm not a member there. I was at Pi Rho Delta. But I've dropped out now."

"Okay, thanks, Robbie," he said, clasping his hand in a firm handshake that he hoped offered some small measure of encouragement. "I guess that's it for now. Thanks a lot for talking to me."

After he left, LaFleur called Blueray. "Can we get more information on Randall?" he asked.

"Of course," said Blueray. "Meet me at the boat."

Back on campus two hours later, after his session with Blueray, LaFleur made his way back up to Randall's office. As he walked down the hall, he could hear a voice as he neared the office door, which was open. Randall was still there, and at first LaFleur thought he was with someone. He glanced into the office and saw that Randall was on the phone, back to the door. LaFleur waited in the hall a few feet away, listening to the one-sided conversation, all unenthusiastic monosyllables on Randall's part: *yeah; yeah; no; uh-huh.*

While he waited, he went over in his mind what Blueray had found in a SUNY faculty database (*Did you just hack into SUNY, fer crissake??? Sort of, Blueray replied.*) They'd discovered that in spite of the PhD, Randall had managed only a series of short term positions at various schools over the years, none of them lasting long, with no tenure. More significantly, Blueray had managed to uncover the record of a long history of disciplinary actions; though details were not available, LaFleur thought he could guess what that meant. In the latest case, by the timing it looked as if Randall had been forced to resign from his previous position—he'd left in the middle of a term. Even more ominously, Blueray had somehow managed to locate a report of a major fire in the chemistry lab of the school Randall had just left—the day after his presumed firing. And the fraternity certificate LaFleur had noticed in his earlier visit? Pi Rho Delta.

Randall finally hung up; LaFleur waited long enough to make it look like he had not been right outside, then knocked on the open door as he walked in. Randall looked up, startled.

"Professor Rand—" LaFleur began.

"You again? What is it? Listen, I don't know anything about any chat room, or Internet, or whatever, I already told you that. What the hell are you bothering me for?"

"I've got some more questions, if you don't mind." The answering scowl probably would have deterred anyone else; LaFleur pressed on. "Specifically, I'm interested in your possible connection to a fraternity fire in 2001, and following that, a fire in the laboratory at SUNY, Buffalo. Certain information has come to light that makes these seeming coincidences—"

"Okay, that's it," barked Randall. "I'm tired of your insinuations. I've got nothing to say to you."

"I can have you re-questioned concerning the recent fire. The fire that killed Amy Polwicz."

"Bullshit." He pushed his chair back angrily and stood up. He started towards LaFleur, as if to push him out of the office. "I don't know why I let you in here in the first place; you're not even a real cop anymore. You live down at the marina, right? Hang out at the bar down there all the time. Well, I don't have to talk to you. And I have no idea why you think you have a right to talk to me at all, as a matter of fact, especially since the police don't think they have any reason to talk to me. There's nothing more to say about it.

I'm sorry it happened, she was a nice girl. But that's it." He moved closer, leaning into LaFleur. "You can go now."

LaFleur stared at him for a few seconds, gauging a response. He realized he didn't have one. He started out the door, then stopped and turned to look back at Randall. "By the way. I was never just a 'cop.' I was a detective."

He left and went back down the hall, footsteps echoing as hollowly as the feeling in the pit of his stomach. Why had he made that crack about not being "just a cop?" In spite of his past frustration with a lot of the less conscientious members of the force, he had never considered himself to be that kind of elitist. God, he felt lousy. Even lousier than usual, if that was possible.

On the way out of the building he passed by a large set of double doors; he'd noticed them on the way in, hadn't paid any attention, but something caught his eye this time—the sign on the door read "Chemistry Lab 104A." He went back and tested the door; it was open. He pushed his way in.

It was pretty much what he had expected a chemistry lab to look like; rows of high counters set with double sinks, racks running along the backs of the counters, with various kinds of glass beakers, retorts, Bunsen burners, other stuff he didn't recognize, all arranged neatly on each counter. Must not be much going on in here at the moment, too orderly, he thought. *So, where would they keep the diethyl ether?*

He walked to the back of the lab; rows of chemicals were arranged on shelves, in no apparent order, at least to his non-chemist mind. He didn't see anything labeled "ether." He noticed a large door in the corner of the lab. He walked over and tried the doorknob, thinking it could be a storeroom. It was unlocked. Just as he was about to push the door open, he heard someone behind him.

"Can I help you?"

Shit. He turned around to see a young guy with a crew cut and tortoiseshell glasses standing behind him, hands on his hips. *Double shit.*

"Uh, hi, um, no, I was…well, nosing around, actually. I was just talking to Professor Randall, upstairs, and, well, I was just curious about the lab, you know."

"Did he give you permission to come in here?" He actually pointed at LaFleur accusingly as he said this.

"Well, no, not exactly, it didn't come up. But we had been talking about various chemicals, lab procedures, that kind of thing, and I just, well, wanted to take a look. I didn't touch anything. Be scared to."

"I think we should go upstairs and—"

"No, no," LaFleur said hastily, "that's not necessary. I was just leaving." He hurried past the kid, who had his hands back on his hips, and, in the best manner of the cheap novels he read occasionally, beat a hasty retreat.

As soon as he was safely back in his car, he called Maggie and let her know he was on his way back to the boat. She said she'd meet him there, but he changed his mind and told her he'd be at Patz instead. Nursing a Grouse.

CHAPTER 15

"Talked to Robbie this afternoon," LaFleur said in a low voice.

Maggie stared straight ahead, waiting for him to continue. They were sitting at a corner table, backs to the bar.

"He seems to be taking it pretty well, considering that, well…" he continued lamely. "Hell. No. He's a wreck. Padre's doing a lot for him, I know, but Robbie's going to need all the help he can get. I tried to take it as easy on him as I could, but just couldn't avoid…"

He gritted his teeth and looked away for a moment, composing himself. "We only talked a few minutes, but you were right; it was enough to convince me to talk to Randall again. So I went back."

"And?"

"I don't know." He drained his scotch, twisted back and held the glass toward the bar for Nikki to see; she noticed it right away and nodded, and nodded again after he realized that Maggie's wine glass was empty as well and signaled *two*.

"It didn't really go all that well," he said, "which I'll go ahead and admit is probably the understatement of the year, but I'm not entirely convinced he's involved. Yes," he said, holding up a hand as she started to object, "I strongly suspect that there was something fishy going on with Amy. I don't doubt Randall'd taken advantage of her, or at least tried to, he seems the type. Robbie was convincing, as I said. There's no doubt that there was quite a bit of bad feeling extremely bad feeling—among the three of them."

"Robbie told you about the fight? The threats? The intimidation? It went on for weeks. They were afraid to leave the apartment."

"Yes, Randall admitted to some of that. But his version is that it was Robbie who instigated it, that nothing had ever happened between him and Amy, and that he was really sorry there had been a dispute over the grade. But Randall claims that is all there was to it, that Robbie blew it all out of proportion. So, yes, I think it's possible, maybe even probable, that Randall has a hand in it somehow. But unless we can get something more on him we're at a dead end."

"So, get more."

"Are you sure you are not just—"

"There has to be more."

"But Randall said—"

"Probably lying."

"C'mon, be reasonable."

"Tell that to Amy."

He knew when he was beaten. "Okay. I'll see what more I can do. Maybe there is something else; maybe we haven't looked hard enough at this guy."

"Thank you."

"Yeah."

They sat in silence for a few seconds.

"Have to admit there seem to be a lot of coincidences," LaFleur said, echoing his earlier conversation at the bar. "Which I generally don't believe in. We—Michael, the Padre and I—we talked about all this quite a bit the other night. Just going to be hard to prove anything, and the official investigations are 'closed,' or as well as closed, even if they claim otherwise. But we've got a lot of different fires at different times and we're finding similarities, connections, that we think are real. So we're not done by a long shot."

"And Randall?" asked Maggie.

"You might be right, Randall could be a key to all this. I guess I have more suspicions than I am ready to allow. But I will definitely keep digging."

Something caught the corner of his eye. Nikki, LaFleur noticed, was standing behind them with the drinks.

"Ah, Nikki. Thanks. In the 'nick' of time. So to speak."

"Ha," said Nikki.

They stayed late, lingering over a Chocolate Mousse "Martini"—one of Pat's creations—and a Frangelico. Most of the staff had been sent home a hour or so early. It had been an unusually slow night; just Pat, the bartender, and the dishwashers in back were there to take care of the two or three remaining patrons and close up.

On the slow walk back to the boat, LaFleur finished describing the photo analysis that he and Michael had

92

started. Maggie felt a chill as he told her how they had both seen the symbols at once. And how they had then gone back and forth over what they meant. Just a coincidence, or a message? If some sort of message or signature, was it strictly fraternity related—meaning Phi Rho Delta—or intended to mean only "pyro?" Or both? Or neither, LaFleur had to admit—although they hadn't come up with any other explanations.

Maggie pointed out immediately something they had already considered: if intended as a mark for Phi Rho Delta fraternity, who indeed had a presence at SUNY, why would the "Delta" be missing? So, they agreed that pyromania was the most likely connotation, but still couldn't rule out some other association. He also went over what he had learned from Debra Gallatin about accelerants and arson in general. He didn't think it necessary to mention that the conversation had been over dinner; that didn't seem relevant.

They had almost reached the boat by now. He was just about to bring up the subject of Michael's confession—and Michael's subsequent decision to ask Nikki out—when he was distracted by motion up ahead of them.

"Hey!" He dropped Maggie's hand and ran towards the boat. Someone—slight build, long, dark hair—had jumped down from the houseboat onto the dock and was running the other direction, toward the end of the marina.

"Hey!" he yelled again.

The figure ran down a dock and disappeared, and seconds later they heard the sound of a small motor boat starting up and pulling away. By the time Maggie caught up with LaFleur at the end of the marina, all they could see was a dark silhouette on the water, heading out toward the lighthouse.

They went back to the boat. The door was still locked, and there were no other signs of a forced entry. Whoever had been on the boat had been scared off before they had a chance to break in. LaFleur unlocked the door and motioned Maggie inside.

"Damn kids," he muttered.

CHAPTER 16

Charlie Case listened to the police and fire scanners the way most people listen to talk radio. There was a scanner in the kitchen that he could hear from the living room, and another next to his bed. He called LaFleur as soon as he heard the calls come over the fire frequency that morning. Another fire, this one in the college bookstore, right downtown.

LaFleur was there in ten minutes. In the crowd he spotted Arlene; the comic shop was only a few storefronts away. They stood and watched as the smoke pouring out of the upper story windows turned from black to white, an indication that a lot of water was hitting the fire.

"Ironic, huh?" Arlene commented.

"What's that?" asked LaFleur.

"The fraternity boys living in the apartments above the store. And now another fire. They had to move out of the fraternity house after the fire?" she prompted.

"Ah. Right. Yes, that is ironic." *More than ironic*, he was beginning to believe. They were going to have to take a closer look at this one. He'd have to call Amos.

A cop came towards them from across the street, waving people off the sidewalk as he approached. "Hey, Falco," LaFleur said as he reached them. "What's it look like this time?"

"Hey, LaFleur. How's it going?"

"Alright. So, what's the deal here, another arson fire?"

Falco shrugged. "Don't ask me, that's out of my pay grade." He turned to look back at the fire. "Hell of a shame, huh? My kid was working at the bookstore for the summer. Now I suppose he'll be screwing around down at the lake every day instead." He turned back and started down the street, half-heartedly moving people along.

After walking Arlene back to the comic shop, LaFleur headed over to Patz. As he made his way into the bar he saw that, as usual, Nikki was talking to Michael, who had arrived earlier. Maggie had gone back to Syracuse for the day to run errands. She was going to do some shopping on the way back; she was making dinner on the boat that night, for just her and LaFleur, for a change.

"Hi, Nikki," he said, squirming his way past her into the booth. "Nothing for me today, thanks," he said as he sat down. Michael, looking embarrassed, said he'd already ordered LaFleur's usual lunch of fried squid and a Saranac. He'd been there waiting quite awhile, he said, apologetically.

LaFleur apologized in return. "Sorry I'm late. Just came from the scene of another fire."

"A fire?" Nikki asked.

"Downtown. At the bookstore."

"Oh, no. Not River's End?" said Michael.

"No, the college bookstore."

"Oh, well, that's a relief. Well, not for the college store, I mean a relief for River's End and for Bill and Mindy... I mean, not a relief, they certainly won't be happy at someone else's misfortune—"

"I know what you mean," said LaFleur. "I talked to Bill for a couple of minutes. He said fire is their greatest worry, even with insurance. What a nightmare it would be to replace all the stock. Not to mention the thought of books burning, he said that just gives him the creeps."

"Not surprising. He loves books." He paused. "Anybody hurt in this one?"

"No, not that I know of, not according to Arlene, anyway. Maggie will be glad to hear that."

"Me, too," said Nikki suddenly. Michael and LaFleur looked at her expectantly, waiting for her to elaborate.

"Well, you know, yeah. I'm glad to hear that." She turned away quickly. "I'll have your orders right out," she said as she walked off.

The bartender—Dave, an ex-cop working part time to supplement his pension—brought over their beers.

"Say, Dave," LaFleur said, "know anything about all the fires lately? You still in touch downtown?"

"Nah, I steer clear these days. I don't think Antonito was sorry to see me go, and I don't want to remind him of anything he might still hold against me."

"The Chief? Why should you be worried about that? You were a great cop."

"Things have changed since you left, A.C."

"So I hear. Well, thanks anyway. If you do hear anything…?"

"You'll be the first."

Michael raised his beer as Dave walked away. "Cheers." LaFleur raised his glass and drank with him.

"So, things are a little hinky at the station these days, huh?" Michael commented.

"I'm starting to think so," LaFleur answered. "Well, hinkier than usual. Anyway, I guess that's part of why Maggie is anxious to get another perspective on this thing. Just wish it didn't have to be me."

"If not you…"

"Yeah, spare me."

***

"Hello, Mr. LaFleur," someone called out.

Maggie had just returned from Syracuse; she and LaFleur were just going into the boat, carrying two bags of groceries. Looking out at the marina over his shoulder, LaFleur saw a good-looking woman in running shorts and a sports bra walking toward them. As she got closer, and as he and Maggie stepped back up onto the pier, he finally recognized her. It was Debra Gallatin.

"I got your message," she said. When LaFleur didn't answer immediately, she prompted, "For dinner tomorrow night? You said you have more questions."

Uncharacteristically flustered—*now, there's a woman who looks comfortable in her skin*, he had been thinking—LaFleur looked over at Maggie before turning back to Debra. "Oh, yeah. Uh, Maggie, this is the arson investigator I told you about. Uh, Debra Gallatin, Maggie Malone." A

98

quick "pleased to meet you" was exchanged, along with significant glances.

"I wondered if we could talk about a few things," continued LaFleur. "Especially since there's been another fire—are you investigating that too, by the way?" he finished lamely.

"No, that's not one of ours," she said. "But I'm glad I caught you. I'm sorry, but I can't make dinner tomorrow, I'm actually leaving in the morning."

LaFleur looked uncomfortable as he shifted his bag of groceries and asked, "Well, how about joining us for dinner here tonight?"

It was a testament to Maggie's extreme good nature that she simply smiled and said, "Yes, Debra, please join us."

"Gosh, Thanks, Maggie. Listen, I'll just run back to the hotel, shower and change, and be back here in, say, thirty minutes?"

Dishes had been stowed and they were gathered up on the sun deck. LaFleur poured three glasses of Limoncello.

"Most people don't realize it," Debra was saying as LaFleur passed around the drinks, "but arson is the second leading cause of fire-related death in this country, after smoking. Over five hundred deaths per year, typically. Arson also ranks second in property damage, running into billions. And most arsonists are never caught—only about fifteen, maybe twenty percent of investigations actually lead to an arrest. And of those who *are* apprehended, the conviction rate is appallingly low, only about two or three percent. Evidence that can stand up in court is very hard to come by."

"How do you manage to catch anyone, if it's that hard?" Maggie asked.

"Every fire—every arsonist, actually—has a unique 'signature,' or what I often call a 'firesign,'" Debra explained. "Serial arsonists in particular have a distinct profile, comprised of a common set of conditions and elements that can be used to construct a signature. Fires are usually set within a relatively small geographic area, for example. Inside the building, the ignition point is often in the same room, using the same accelerant. Fires are typically set around the same time; two in the morning seems to be a popular time."

"About the same time that the pizza parlor caught fire," LaFleur said.

"Yes, that's right," Debra said, nodding as she continued. "Other factors include gender and age—white males make up ninety percent of convicted arsonists, with over half under twenty years old. Previous criminal behavior is also a large factor; one-quarter have prior arrest records."

"So you take all of these factors into account when investigating every fire?" LaFleur asked. "A lot of considerations."

"Exactly," relied Debra. "Of course, not every signature contains every element I've described. But you can't afford to overlook any one element. You have to be careful and patient. You have to read the firesigns correctly. And even if you do, there's no guarantee that the signs will lead to your arsonist. Justice is not often found in these cases."

"And the pizza parlor fire?" he asked. "Arson?"

Debra grimaced. "Sorry," she said. "Can't really say…"

"So, still no resolution," said LaFleur, dejectedly. "Well, I'm used to that."

He sighed and poured everyone another Limoncello.

100

CHAPTER 17

Blueray came early; he'd nearly bumped into Maggie as she left the boat on her way out. He gave LaFleur a knowing look as he sat down at the computer and started to comment; LaFleur cut him off with a slight squint and an almost imperceptible shake of his head. Blueray sat down quickly and booted up the system.

It wasn't too long before he called to LaFleur over his shoulder: "Detective. Found something!"

LaFleur came in from the galley carrying a cup of coffee and bent over to look at the computer screen. All he saw was a big list of incomprehensible numbers. Blueray had several other small windows open around the screen, pointing out specific items to LaFleur.

"Here's another one of your pyro chat room guys," he said.

"Ah, I was afraid you found a hacker."

"No, far as I can tell, we're clean. Well, a little while ago I thought I had found an attack, but it turned out to be nothing. But look at this guy," he said, highlighting an entry. "Goes by the name of 'Vesuvius' online. Real name's Roger Milhouse. What a dweeb. And look at this." Blueray clicked an icon. "Facebook."

This was all new to LaFleur. He had never seen a Facebook page in his life. Was proud of the fact. But it went to show that you should never limit your options. Damn good thing he had asked Blueray to help out. "So, anything interesting there?" he asked.

"Would you call this 'interesting?'" Blueray said, pushing into another page. Pictures of the recent fires, both the pizza parlor and the bookstore. And at the bottom of the page, one of a bus stop shelter burning, apparently in the middle of the night, no one around.

Blueray looked up at LaFleur. "Want his home address?" he asked.

This could get me in a hell of a lot of trouble, LaFleur said to himself as he walked up to the house. The Milhouses lived on the edge of the downtown area, in a small, somewhat dilapidated white house. Needed paint more than anything. LaFleur went to the side of the house first, looking around quickly before going to the front door. The back yard was a large, barren area, a couple of piles of junk stacked up in one corner. There were some suspiciously blackened spots near one pile of old crates. Probably jumping to conclusions, he told himself. Never preset expectations.

He went to the door, didn't see a doorbell, so knocked on the screen door, which rattled loudly in the frame. Out of the corner of his eye he saw a curtain in the front window pull back, then drop closed again. There was still no sound from inside. The door opened a crack just as he started banging on the screen door again.

"Oh, hello. Sorry." He leaned over to peer in at the face behind the door. It was a young kid, late teens, probably. Roger. Good, no parents at home today. "I'm looking for Roger Milhouse?"

The face moved a little closer to the opening in the door, enough for LaFleur to make out a doughy face framed by stringy, dark hair.

"Yeah?"

"Are you Roger?"

"Yeah. What do you want?"

"I have some questions for you." He reached into his pocket and pulled out a black wallet, thinking to fake the kid out by flashing it open, then thought better of it and put it away. He saw Roger glance at it nervously, however—the ploy had worked, even if unintentionally.

"There have been some fires in the area recently," LaFleur continued. "You participate in an online 'discussion group' that's related to fire, isn't that right?"

After a long silence, Roger replied. "I guess so."

"There is evidence that you may have been involved in one or more of those fires."

Another silence, then a guarded reply. "What evidence?"

At least he didn't ask *what fires*. "A series of photographs. Posted on your Facebook page."

"Oh, shit. Listen, man, I didn't take those pictures," he said defensively.

"Who did?"

"One of the guys in the chat. He offered to send them to me, I didn't even know what he was sending."

"But you posted them on your page. You like fires?"

Roger finally started to balk. "Hey, I don't have to answer unless you have a warrant, right?"

"That's just for searches. I'm just asking for information at the moment." He paused. "Do you have a computer here? Or do you use one at SUNY?"

"Oh, crap. Hey. Listen, man," Roger said in a now quavering voice. "I just thought the pictures were cool, okay? I don't really have much to do with those guys in that group. I was just, well…"

"Can you give me their names?"

"I only know one of them. He was in my class. Uh, Louie. Louie Delgado."

" 'Screwy Louie?' "

Roger blanched at this, like *how did he know*? "Yeah. That's right. Hey, I really don't know what—"

"Do you know how serious this is? Someone died, you know. That's not just arson, that's murder."

"Oh, God. Oh, God. We didn't do anything, honest to God we didn't. We just fool around online, you know? We…we…" He started to sob.

"Okay, okay," LaFleur interrupted. He waited a moment until the sobbing subsided. The door opened slightly wider. "I think you're telling me the truth," he went on in a sincere tone. "Listen, I can't promise anything, but since you've been cooperative, and if this Louie character gives me what I want, you could be off the hook. I might not even have to take you in for questioning." *As if I could anyway*.

"Oh, man, that would be great. Really, man, I really, uh…"

"Don't mention it." LaFleur turned to walk away. "Don't contact Louie."

"Oh, no, man, I wouldn't..." His voice faded as LaFleur made his way out to the street and got into his car. Roger watched from the crack in the door until he drove away.

Next stop was home for a quick lunch. While he ate a turkey sandwich, he called the station, hoping Amos was in. After running the usual bureaucratic gauntlet, the dispatcher finally connected him.

"Hey. It's me. Need a favor."

"Yeah, why doesn't that surprise me? You know, you always make me feel like Sgt. Becker on *The Rockford Files*. So, what can I do for you, 'Jim?'"

"Funny. So, remember a kid by the name of Louie Delgado? Five years ago or so. We picked him up on a burglary charge, he was only twelve or thirteen. He was put up to it by an older guy, an uncle or somebody like that."

"Yeah, that high school thing?"

"Right. The older guy was a janitor at Oswego High. Sent the kid in through a small window at a school district warehouse to steal janitorial supplies. Then the guy would sell them back to the school."

"Yeah, and no one could figure it out for the longest time. You finally did that one on your own, didn't you?"

"Yeah. Everyone knew something was fishy, but no one was willing to take the time to figure it out. Not that it did any good; guy didn't even lose his job, as I recall. Still, I had the satisfaction. All you get, sometimes. But anyway, I need the kid's current whereabouts."

"Give me ten."

"You're a prince."

"I know. Talk to you in a few minutes, Jim."

Amos never did know when to let a joke drop.

It was more like thirty minutes, but Amos came back with an address, and with some recent charges on his sheet that LaFleur hadn't known about. Among other random acts of vandalism and some petty theft, Louie had been picked up a couple of years earlier while setting fire to an abandoned tool shed; it was obviously just malicious mischief and not what Amos would term "serious" arson—juvie court sentenced him to picking up litter for a few days. Over the long term, the juvenile justice system had not been successful in rehabilitating Louie Delgado; he was still in and out of court like it had a revolving door, Amos said—you name it, he's been in for it.

LaFleur promised Amos a lunch someday, then headed back out.

Louie Delgado lived in one side of a rundown duplex in Fulton. He was apparently on his own; Amos didn't have any current information on parents or other next of kin. There was no doorbell, so LaFleur rapped on the small window in the door with his ring. For the second time that day, his luck held; Louie was home. And as soon as Louie opened the door, LaFleur recognized him—he hadn't changed since the high school burglaries—same short, skinny, pale wreck he'd been five years ago, same stringy hair, but longer now. He was dressed like Roger Milhouse in ragged jeans and a black heavy metal themed t-shirt.

"You!" Louie exclaimed as he opened the door, obviously also recognizing LaFleur. "What the hell do you want? I ain't done nothin'."

Could have predicted that, LaFleur thought. *Surprised he didn't say 'ya lousy copper.'*

"Maybe not. But you might have information I need."

"I just told you, I don't know nothin'."

"Well, you actually said 'I ain't *done* nothin.' But that's not really true. You sent pictures of some recent fires to one of your pyromaniac friends."

Louie didn't flinch. "So what. Against the law to take pictures?"

"You took them, then? You were at the fires?"

"I didn't say I took them." This was said with such an incongruous air of superiority that LaFleur almost laughed out loud.

"Well, that's not what I'm really interested in, anyway," he continued. "You know anyone goes by the name of 'Fudd' in your little online group? Any teachers or anyone else at SUNY who's involved?"

"Hey, you know what? This is boring. I don't know nothin', I ain't done nothin', and you're startin' to piss me off." The door slammed.

***

"Don't you ever take a day off?" Michael asked Nikki, as she greeted them near the bar. LaFleur had called a "dinner meeting."

"Can't afford it," she said; her hand automatically went to Michael's shoulder as he sat down. LaFleur winked at him, out of Nikki's line of sight; Michael had told him earlier that his first date with Nikki—they'd gone out to a movie the night before last—had gone pretty well, considering.

"You'll own this place before long," Father Tommy said to Nikki as he settled onto a stool next to Michael.

"Oh, no, she won't," said Pat, coming up behind them. "In fact, she's here so much I'm going to start charging her rent." He laughed. Nikki reached over and hit him with a menu.

"We'll see what Pat has to say about that," she said, trying to sound menacing. "Anyway, it's these three who should be paying rent. They're in here all the time, lately."

"Business," said LaFleur.

"What business?" mocked Nikki. "You've been off the force for years. Or, what, someone hire you as a night guard for their boat?"

"Actually," said Tommy theatrically, "we're investigating the fires."

Pat's eyebrows arched. "Really? There's something going on that we don't know about? From what I read in the paper, not much was happening with the investigations. Open and shut."

"That's what the departments would have you believe," said Tommy. "But we think there's more to it. A lot more."

"Like what?" Pat asked, as LaFleur tried to signal Tommy. *Shut up,* he mouthed.

"Like certain evidence that is being suppressed," Tommy went on obliviously. He seemed to be enjoying this.

Michael took up the narrative, spurred by Tommy's air of mystique and equally oblivious to LaFleur's growing discomfort. "Not to mention some very strange graffiti we detected in some photos of—"

"Nothing significant," LaFleur abruptly said, before they could go on. His instinct for protecting the confidentiality of a case had been one of the things that had made him so successful as a detective. Never give anything away, in any circumstance, even if you think it won't matter. It almost always did matter, maybe in a small way, maybe in an important way. But it always mattered. You couldn't know how or why something might compromise an investigation, not until it was too late.

"But—" "Well, we did—" Michael and the Father said at once.

"I'm sure the department has it well under control," LaFleur interrupted, again.

Pat looked disappointed, but nodded. "Well, if you hear of anything…"

"You'll be…"

"…the first to know," Pat completed for him laughing. "So, Nikki," he said, looking over his shoulder for her, "when will a table open up for these gentlemen?"

He turned back and shrugged. "Now where did she run off to? If she wants to own this place someday, she'll have to do better than that."

As he left, LaFleur glared at Father Tommy and Michael. "Either of you ever heard the term 'discretion?' We need to be at least a little careful with this. Me in particular. You guys've got nothing to lose, I guess, but I have a reputation in this town—did have a reputation—and I don't need to be seen as a crackpot running around making trouble. There is, remember, supposedly, an official investigation still going on. An insurance arson investigator is here. Let's not stir up a hornet's nest. You know what this town is like, should change the name to Gossip City. And Pat sees *everyone* in here, sooner or later." They looked appropriately mollified.

"So, I was thinking about fraternities," he said, settling himself onto a stool next to Tommy. He didn't get far before the bartender—someone new, LaFleur observed—came over with the standard "what'll it be?"

"Ah, Famous Grouse all round, thanks." The bartender nodded and reached back to pull down the bottle. LaFleur leaned back, looking from Father Tommy to Michael. "Odd thing," he said, "the fire in the bookstore? Frat boys living upstairs. And the pizza fire a few weeks ago—the apartment upstairs, the one Amy was in?—that was the boyfriend's apartment, right? And he was in a fraternity. Guess which one?"

"Here you go, guys," said the barman, spreading out the three glasses of scotch.

"Thanks," replied LaFleur absentmindedly, as the three of them raised their glasses. "Cheers. Well, here's where I am on all this so far," LaFleur went on. "We're looking for an arson signature—a 'firesign,' to use Debra Gallatin's term—that identifies a particular individual as our arsonist. Seemingly unrelated factors that might in fact mark someone as the arsonist, if when added together they make up a unique signature. Or items that either look related, or are in fact known to be related, these can also add up to a signature. So we need to look at each of our possibles in those terms." He paused to sip at his scotch, then continued.

"All the fires possibly, but so far unproven to be, arson. All with apartments above. The two college kids hurt in the 1998 fire? Both fraternity members.

"Michael, I forgot to tell you; that Reen character? According to Amos, he's been a suspect in more than one fire, but never convicted, never even charged. Oh, yeah, Padre, do you remember, it was years ago, there was an arson attempt on a fraternity house—don't know which one, we can check on that—there was a lot of publicity centered around an accusation made against a local crazy named Reen. Nicknamed 'Matchstick,' after the old match factory." Father Tommy vaguely remembered something like that. "So, maybe we keep him on the list, but I don't

110

believe in coincidences like that; too pat. I just can't put him at all these fires. He's just a harmless kook. No signature at all, really."

"I still think you should go talk to him, A.C.," said Michael, leaning in. "I've told you what we say at the hospital—if you hear horses' hooves, don't diagnose zebras."

"I'll keep that in mind next time I'm looking for zebras," LaFleur said. "Or would that be if I were looking for horses? Never mind. But you're right, I'll go talk to him. We go way back, maybe there's some intimidation factor still left there that I can use. Where was I? The pyro-wannabe kids I'm not too worried about. I just talked to two of them—thanks to Blueray's Internet sleuthing—and I'm pretty sure they're a dead end. Same thing—they have some of the right elements, you can build a signature for them, but it's the wrong signature. Doesn't match our fires. Losers, for sure, and one of them is capable of about anything, and he *really* dislikes me, but we've really got nothing solid on them. Unless something else turns up implicating them, I'm moving them to the bottom of the list. With the zebras." He paused while Michael made threatening gestures.

"On a more serious note," he went on, "there's the chemistry professor and the coed. Maggie insisted that I go and talk to Randall again. She's convinced that Randall's hiding something. That I'm not ready to call either way; but there are indications that Randall could be involved. But so far, he's got the strongest signature of the group."

LaFleur ticked off a list of factors supporting his case. "He's familiar with the chemistry of one of the accelerants known to have been used in at least one of the fires. He was living in proximity to more than one of the fires, including

111

one in his own lab, and has an association with the Pi Rho Delta fraternity. He's been accused, though not convicted, of a potential felony. He has a background of disciplinary action. He's the right age, the right gender, the right ethnicity. He fits the profile. And he has—had—a serious conflict with one of the victims."

"So you're saying we might have some solid evidence?" Tommy said. "Something specifically related to Amy's fire?"

"Well. Maybe I'm getting ahead of myself. Still a lot of variables. And no clear motives, not in all cases." He sat back and looked up at the ceiling, immediately reconsidering. "*But*," he continued, "if the pizza fire—the new pizza fire, the one that killed Amy—is connected to the bookstore apartment fire, and to the other fraternity fire, then we've got something to go on.

"I don't think I've told you yet, Padre; as we were going over the fire photos using Blueray's magic photo enhancement tool, Michael found some ominous looking graffiti on more than one of the burned buildings, the Greek characters 'pi' and 'rho.' Signs of either pyromania, or a link to the fraternity, or both. And we're doing some pretty sophisticated imaging and pattern matching, again thanks to our technical guru. I think it's just a matter of time before—"

"Sorry to interrupt," Nikki said, who had been standing behind them, "but your table's ready."

It happened on the way out of Patz.

Michael was over by the bar talking to Nikki. LaFleur and Father Tommy were already in the foyer near the front door, waiting for him. Nikki was laughing at something Michael said, then turned her head to look over at them. As they watched, she suddenly blanched, her face instantly becoming pale and twisted, and she dropped the tray of drinks she was holding.

Distracted by the noise of the tray and glasses crashing to the floor, LaFleur and Tommy didn't notice that someone had just come in the front door. They both went over to Nikki and Michael; Michael was holding Nikki by the shoulders, nearly holding her up, as she stared at the entrance. As they all stood there, wondering what to do, Nikki suddenly broke away from Michael and ran into the kitchen. Before anyone could react to that, LaFleur heard someone call out his name. He turned to look over at the front door, where Nikki had just been so intently staring a few seconds earlier.

It was Lance Randall.

"LaFleur!" Randall called out again.

Mother Mary help us, what does this clown want? LaFleur spun around to face Randall. Michael took off after Nikki. Tommy stood watching in confusion.

"Professor...?" LaFleur was having a hard time focusing.

"What's the big idea, LaFleur?"

Shaking his head, LaFleur could only offer a weak, "What do you mean?"

"My post-doc just told me that he found you wandering around in my lab. What the hell did you think you were doing?"

"I was just curious. Since we—"

"Ah—save it, LaFleur. Just stay away from me, just stay away. Got that?" He turned and walked out.

"Jumping Jesus, A.C.," said Father Tommy. "What was that all about? And what happened to Nikki and Michael?"

CHAPTER 18

Michael caught up with Nikki behind the restaurant. She was hunched over, hands on her knees. She looked up at him as he came around the corner.

"Leave me alone."

He stopped, holding out his hands, an offering.

"It's LaFleur's fault that Randall came in here, isn't it?" Nikki demanded.

Michael didn't answer; LaFleur had said that his last encounter with Randall hadn't been a good one, but he didn't really know any more than that.

Nikki looked back down at the ground, then straightened and looked over at Michael. "Tell him to stay out of it, Michael." She turned and walked away.

Later that night, back at Nikki's, Michael implored her to talk to him about it. She reluctantly told him the story. Some of it, anyway. By turns morose and angry, she related, in bits and pieces, what had caused her to "flip out," as she said, when she saw Randall at Patz. She didn't know he was in Oswego again, she said. She hadn't seen him since...well, for years.

Michael was doing his best to console her, which didn't seem to be working, since he didn't know what he was consoling her *for*. She sat quietly next to him for a time, her head on his shoulder, but then she was up, pacing. She'd known Randall from community college, she explained, he had been teaching a course there. She'd started seeing him; had gone to a couple of fraternity parties. Then one night...but at that she flopped down on the sofa next to him and fell silent.

"What's the deal with LaFleur?" she asked suddenly after a few minutes. "Why is he talking about fires all the time? With you and Father Tommy."

Michael wasn't sure how to answer this, given that LaFleur was worried about spreading too much information around. He just explained that LaFleur was looking into a particular fire as a favor to Maggie and that had led to other cases.

"He's going after Randall, isn't he?"

"Well, there is some reason to believe that he might be involved somehow."

"He has no idea," she said.

What the hell? Michael thought. "Listen, if there's something you know..."

"No, forget it." She closed her eyes and put her hands behind her head. "There was a big mix-up with a food service order the other day," she said. "Someone at Sysco

Foods called and asked for "Pat," and he answered, but the person at Sysco had talked to "she-Pat," not "he-Pat," and Pat didn't have any idea what they were talking about, and they ended up sending…" She abruptly dropped her story, before getting to the punch line, and went back to how Randall had ruined her chances to get a nursing diploma. And worse, she said vehemently, but didn't elaborate.

"What are you doing tomorrow, are you going to see LaFleur again?" she asked, raising her head and looking up at him, again switching topics without warning. "Tell him to stay out of it," she said for the third time, before he could answer. "Or else I will," she added as an afterthought.

Then she appeared to change gears again, softening her voice and apologizing for losing control at the restaurant, and for being such a bitch. It had just been such a shock, she said. He said he understood. They stayed on the couch, snuggling a bit while she seemed to relax; she even nodded off for a few minutes. There was some more snuggling.

Soon the couch became much too narrow.

"Ummm….uh uh."

She pushed his arm away, gently, as he reached down and started to pull up her chemise from the bottom. It was very low cut, the top held up only by the thinnest of spaghetti strings. It barely covered her breasts to begin with—it was now half off, but she obviously didn't mind.

"Hmmm?" Michael said lazily, raising up on one elbow, again reaching down and gently sliding his hand under the silk, which began to pull the chemise up over her thighs.

"Michael! No, I said!" she said, brusquely slapping his hands away this time and turning her back to him. "Please don't." She sat up. "I prefer it this way." She reached up

116

and pulled the top half down, leaving it draped around her waist. "How's this?"

He laid back down, perplexed, but accommodating.

Before she turned back to him, he glimpsed what looked like a small tattoo, just at the base of her spine, half covered by the lingerie. Butterflies? And some foreign characters—Chinese, or maybe Japanese—embedded in the center of the pattern.

"Is that a tattoo on your back?" he asked. "What is it? Some kind of good luck symbol or something?"

Nikki didn't answer, simply shaking her head and looking at him crossly. As she climbed on top of him, he forgot all about it.

CHAPTER 19

Early the next morning, LaFleur drove over to Elihu Reen's. He sensed that Michael wasn't going to let this rest until LaFleur had talked to Reen; might as well get it over with. He still thought it was too much of a long shot.

Reen's house was a dilapidated two-story on East Sixth, unusual only in the amount of paint peeling from the wooden siding. The porch looked as if it might fall off any second; LaFleur held on to a shaky rail as he made his way up to the front door.

The disheveled old man who answered the door looked more like Icabod Crane than LaFleur had remembered. Skinny as a rail, LaFleur had described him to Michael, but that did not do justice to the stick figure now standing in front of him. In spite of it being mid-summer, Reen was dressed in an old grey sweat suit, which looked about four sizes too large. Lank hair strung out in a random pattern over a greasy bald head completed the package.

"Yeah?" Reen squeaked through the screen door.

"Hello, Mr. Reen," LaFleur said politely, suppressing a laugh. *Even his voice is skinny.*

"Yeah?" Reen repeated, his voice pitched even higher.

"Don't remember me, Mr. Reen? Detective LaFleur. Though I'm now retired."

Reen peered through the shabby door, eyes squinting like a distressed pig. "Yeah, I remember you alright," he said. "Now that you put a name to that ugly kisser of yours. Yeah, I remember you alright." Reen shifted his weight from one foot to the other in a weird kind of shuffle, while holding his hands to his head. "What do you want?" he whined.

Taken aback by the strange appearance and even stranger behavior, LaFleur momentarily forgot what it was he was doing there.

"What, what, what?" Reen chanted, still moving his feet back and forth.

LaFleur stepped back a step or two, holding up his hands. "Don't get upset, Mr. Reen. I just wanted to ask you about something. Something that happened many years ago. Nothing to worry about, just looking for some information."

This seemed to appease Reen somewhat. He stopped shuffling, but otherwise didn't respond. LaFleur repeated that he was just looking for information. Reen began to open the screen door and LaFleur felt a sudden dread—he was actually going to ask him into the house! Thankfully, the door opened only a few inches, as Reen stuck his skeletal visage out through the crack.

"If it's about that shopping cart, I'll take it back."

"No, no. Nothing like that."

Reen let the screen door close, much to LaFleur's relief. "Well, what then?"

Should I even go through with this? LaFleur thought, before finally asking, "Do you remember, Mr. Reen, several years ago, there was a fire at a fraternity house not far from here?"

"I was cleared!" Reen screeched. "I was cleared. Not me! Not me!" He began shuffling again, faster this time, and suddenly pulled his sweat shirt up over his head.

"Okay, okay," said LaFleur quickly. "I believe you." He turned halfway away from the door and looked in at Reen, who was practically dancing at this point. "I believe you," he said again, then turned around and hurried back to the car.

I should have sent Michael over here, he thought as he drove away. *He'll never believe me.*

***

Newton hated to have his late afternoon nap interrupted, and the sound of Blueray entering the boat in his usual bounding style was more traumatic than usual. As Blueray walked by the sofa at the edge of the salon, Newton lowered himself as flat as he could get, looking up anxiously for the next catastrophic event.

"Don't panic, Newton," LaFleur said as he watched from the computer desk. "Only our rambunctious friend." Newton refused to look even slightly mollified, gave Blueray a disgusted look, and slowly settled back in to one corner, still watchful but out of panic mode.

"Sorry, Newton," Blueray said over his shoulder as he swung his backpack to the floor. "Don't be so nervous."

"You're talking about a *cat*, Blueray. They *invented* nervous."

"Well, it's obviously rubbed off on you, if you're suddenly asking for security cameras." As a matter of fact, for the past couple of days LaFleur had been thinking over the disturbance at the boat that night with Maggie—the figure they saw was of slight build, long dark hair—LaFleur thought it might have been that damn Delgado kid.

Blueray pulled a couple of boxes out of his pack and started opening one up. "I got everything we'll need. Nothing too fancy, but it should work fine; and I stayed under budget. The guy at the camera store in Syracuse didn't even check the signature on your credit card. And I thought I did a pretty good job signing, too." He pulled what looked like two large webcams out of one of the boxes, each with an antenna sticking out the top. "Two wireless cameras, battery-powered, night-vision spec'd to be good for over twenty feet, 300 foot wi-fi range. I'll run the output directly onto your external drive, should be plenty of space. We'll check them every day and delete the files as we go. Where do you want the cameras?"

"One up top to scan the dock. One in here; only way in. You say these things have night vision?"

"Yeah. But in here we should leave a small light on. We'll want as good a picture as we can get. If we get anything," he added.

"Sounds like a plan," LaFleur agreed. He picked up a small box. "What's this?"

"Receiver." Blueray took it over to the desk, pulling an AC adapter out of a plastic bag as he went. "Okay, this shouldn't take too long. Got any soda?"

It had taken only about two hours for Blueray to finish setting up the cameras. As soon as he finished loading the software and giving LaFleur some basic instruction, he took off. LaFleur decided that now was a good time to call Amos Brown again.

"Sgt. Becker?" LaFleur said, as Amos answered the phone. LaFleur thought he'd get the joke in first for a change.

"Ha, yeah, Becker here," replied Amos, laughing. "What is it this time, Jimbo?"

"Can you run a name for me? Lance Randall. See if there's anything on him for, oh, say, the last ten years or so."

"Spell it?"

"L-a-n-c-e R-a-n-d-a-double 'l'—Randall. Teaches at SUNY at the moment, not sure where he was before that."

"What's this about, A.C.?"

"Maggie's fire. And I think I just added him to the list of people who for some reason don't like me."

"Yeah, well, that's getting to be a long list. Uh, not sure how soon I can get to this..."

"C'mon. Take you fifteen minutes. Call me back if you get any hits."

He heard back from Amos later that night. He was surprised—and confused—over what Amos told him he'd found.

About twelve years ago, Amos said, Nikki Faghin was assaulted at a local fraternity party. "Date rape," according to the report, but the details in the case record belied that characterization. Christ on a crutch, Amos, LaFleur started in, what the hell are you talking about, and so on, until Amos got him to shut up and listen.

The only name listed in the report as a "possible" was —LaFleur really hated coincidences like this—someone, maybe a fraternity member, named Lance Randall.

However, Amos continued, the case was never prosecuted—in fact, as far as he could tell, Nikki never even reported it to the police; she just went to the hospital E.R., was examined briefly, then left without ever being questioned. The only reason Randall's name was in the police records at all was due to the fact that the hospital was required to make a report on any sexual assault case— but with no charges and no victim, the police wouldn't have been able—or interested—in pursuing it. There was nothing else in the database on Randall—no wants, no priors, just the mention in the hospital report.

Staring at the notes he'd made while talking to Amos, LaFleur realized he didn't really know that much about Nikki, even though he had known her casually at Patz for quite awhile, three or four years. Had never really thought much about her beyond that; she delivered sandwiches to the boat pretty regularly, and they'd had a friendly, bantering relationship at the restaurant, but that was about as far as it went. Until lately, anyway, with the new interest in Michael.

Twelve years...

"Damn it, Newton, this stuff never ends, does it?"

CHAPTER 20

LaFleur called the hospital and asked for Dr. Vito Martin, the doctor listed in the police report. He knew Dr. Martin through Michael and Maggie; it was a small town, and sometimes that paid off. He briefly explained to Martin what he was after. Martin agreed to see him if he could come over right away, even though he said he couldn't promise anything. He told LaFleur to just come up to his office when he got there.

At LaFleur's knock at his open office door, Dr. Martin looked up. "Ah, A.C., come on in. Been awhile."

"Hello, Vito. Yes, it has."

"Since that bad business last year, isn't it?" Dr Martin continued. He was referring to an incident that had taken place at the hospital the previous November. While LaFleur was investigating a cold case at Maggie's request—the supposed suicide of a young nurse named Angie, in 1964—

124

Maggie had nearly been murdered. Dr. Franklin Montgomery, head of Oswego Hospital, had injected her with curare in an attempt to silence her regarding his involvement in illegal abortions and possible involvement in the nurse's death back in '64. Michael Fuentes had intervened at the last second, saving Maggie. Montgomery had died of a massive coronary minutes later after Michael's rescue of Maggie; whether or not he was actually involved in the nurse's death remained a mystery.

"Any word on Mahoney?" Dr. Martin asked. A second suspect, an anesthesiologist who had been involved with the nurse at the time, had vanished to parts unknown.

LaFleur shook his head ruefully. "Nope. Don't know that we'll ever see him again. Or that we'll ever know what really happened back in 1964. But at least we tried."

Martin motioned to LaFleur to take a seat on the other side of his desk. "Well, like I said on the phone, I'm really not sure I can tell you much of anything, A.C.," Martin said apologetically, as LaFleur sat down." You may have wasted your time coming over here."

"I'm not sure I follow you. I already have the police report. I just want to get some background details cleared up."

"What I mean," Martin said, "is that in cases like this we have to be very careful to maintain patient confidentiality," Martin explained. "HIPPA privacy rules don't allow us to disclose patient information except in very specific circumstances."

"But that's just it," said LaFleur. "Since it was never reported as a crime, you're not really bound by the same rules of confidentiality, are you? The same as if, say, there had actually been charges brought, or something like that."

Martin's dubious expression didn't change. "I don't know..." he said, then appeared to reconsider. "I suppose this could come under the 'Abuse' clause." LaFleur leaned forward as Martin continued. "In certain cases of abuse, domestic violence, that kind of thing, we can divulge information to the authorities without prior permission." He paused. "You have the police report, you said? Are you working with the department?"

"Not exactly," LaFleur had to admit. "But I have an agreement with Detective Amos Brown to turn over anything we come up with during the investigation.."

"Well, I suppose we're okay, then" Martin agreed.

"So, tell me exactly what happened that night," LaFleur prompted.

"As you already know," Martin began, "that night a girl came into the E.R. claiming she'd been assaulted, at a fraternity party, I believe. I found out later it was Nikki Faghin. I was called into the E.R. to do the rape kit. She looked terrible—clothes all disheveled, hair a mess—and she was slurring her words, obviously disoriented. Very distraught. We got her into an exam room, up on a table, and I did the examination. We were having a hard time getting her to tell us what had happened to her, and she kept trying to get up off the exam table. I was finally able to calm her down enough to do the exam, quickly, and could tell right away that she'd definitely been, well, violated...she'd had intercourse. She was trying to tell us about someone who'd either been there and had been part of it, but her speech was very disjointed; the only name I was able to recognize was a Randall something. So I think that—"

"You said Randall?" confirmed LaFleur. "Lance Randall?"

"Yes, that's it. Lance Randall."

"Okay. Anybody else, any other names?"

"No, that's the only name I remember."

"Did the kit ever go to the lab?"

"Probably. But since we never processed her, any information that came back subsequently might not have been filed."

Martin sat back in his chair, hesitating. "We get a lot of stuff in here that's pretty disturbing," he resumed, wrapping his arms around himself, "stuff I can't believe sometimes." LaFleur nodded. He'd seen a lot of things he'd rather forget as well. Martin went on grimly. "She'd been burned. Like with a cigarette, or a cigar. One burn looked a lot like a cigarette lighter, little rings, you know, like from an electric car lighter? There were burns in several places, on her inner thighs, her buttocks. And I'm pretty sure that she'd been drugged, probably chlorohydrate, but without doing a urinalysis you can't tell, and of course we didn't get a chance to do that."

"You didn't," LaFleur said, shifting forward onto the edge of his chair, "get a chance?"

"No. While we were preparing to clean her up, getting dressings, burn pads...she jumped off the table, pulled her clothes on, and ran out of the E.R. We never even admitted her."

"So, what then, you made the report to the police?"

"Yeah, I filled out the report and an officer came over later and picked it up. By this time she was long gone."

Before leaving the hospital, LaFleur tried to track down Michael; they were going to have to talk about this, soon. Unfortunately, he was told by the floor nurse that Dr. Fuentes was tied up in surgery, and had a full schedule for the rest of the evening—an elective C-section had been pushed back three hours due to an earlier E.R. case—and on top of that, she told LaFleur, Dr. Fuentes was on call. LaFleur left a message at the nurses' station and went home. Michael never called. LaFleur finally went to bed a little after twelve.

***

While LaFleur slept, fitfully, a plastic jug lay propped up on its side in the engine room. It looked like a milk jug that had been filled with water and frozen—there was no lid on the jug, and the bottle neck was filled with ice.

By about 2 a.m., the ice—and there was only a small plug of ice about an inch or two thick—had melted enough in the warm below-decks compartment to pop out of the top of the jug. Tiny sparks from the motor on the bilge pump— which almost never stopped running—were more than enough to ignite the gallon of ether as it poured out onto the floor.

CHAPTER 21

Michael could barely stay awake as he made the fifteen-minute drive home that night, even though it was only around one. He'd been called to the hospital three nights running and he'd spent nearly all night at the hospital each time. Unlike some anesthesiologists he'd worked with in the past, Michael never left the hospital after giving an epidural—too many possible complications. Not only did he want to avoid any potential malpractice problems, it just wasn't ethical to place the catheter and then go home and go back to bed, leaving it up to the OB nurse to remove it. One of the deliveries the night before had gone on for hours, the mother-soon-to-be demanding the IV one minute, refusing it the next, screaming at him the whole time. Very exhausting for all involved.

The drive home had perversely energized Michael to the point where he knew he would not be able to sleep right away. He was changing into his sweats and deciding if he wanted to go to the trouble to make something to eat when he noticed LaFleur's note—it had fallen out of his shirt pocket onto the floor. He'd forgotten all about it.

Pouring himself a small shot of single malt in the kitchen, he decided it was too late to try to get in touch with LaFleur tonight, even though the note had said it was "important." He'd call first thing in the morning; LaFleur was an early riser.

After fifteen minutes or so, the scotch had done the trick, squelching his appetite and making him drowsy enough to try sleeping. He put the bread and cheese back in the refrigerator and went to bed. His sleep was plagued by strange dreams—hugely pregnant women floating above his bed, scolding him, nurses pulling the women this way and that.

Still dreaming vividly at dawn—he knew in a half-awake state that it was still a dream, since the patient was floating several inches above the hospital bed—he was preparing to place an epidural. As he turned the patient over, he saw a tiny tattoo in the small of her back. He leaned forward, trying to make out the tattoo's design, and fell out of bed. The shock as he hit the floor was caused less by falling out of bed and waking up suddenly than by the sickening realization triggered by the dream—the two characters inked into Nikki's back were not Chinese, or Japanese, or any other Asian language. And the pattern was not a butterfly.

The letters were Greek. And they were surrounded by flames. And LaFleur wasn't answering his phone. He started to leave a message, realized it was more or less incomprehensible, and cut it off mid-sentence.

He had to find LaFleur.

CHAPTER 22

The first explosion didn't even wake LaFleur. Newton, however, was on his feet before the sound of the soft *whoomp,* coming from somewhere in the bowels of the boat, had even died out. He carefully crawled around at the foot of the bed nervously, searching in the dark for whatever had made the unusual sound. LaFleur didn't stir.

Newton's head jerked up at some odd popping noises. He jumped down off of the bed and crept in the direction of the bedroom door, belly dragging on the floor. He stopped and listened, ears turning in opposite directions. He stayed that way for almost a minute, scarcely breathing.

The sound of the second explosion ripped through the boat like a sonic boom. LaFleur woke up. Newton flew back onto the bed as if shot out of a cannon.

"What the—"

Another smaller explosion caused the boat to rock. This was not a good sign. LaFleur was still trying to comprehend what was happening. Then the smell hit him, an acrid throat-burning wave composed of diesel fuel vapors and burning plastic.

He started for the bedroom door, but just as he was about to open it, he saw the dark smoke curling under the bottom of the door, seeping in at the sides.

He stood there dressed only in Dockers pajama bottoms, frozen in place. Newton yowled, a low, alien-sounding screech that LaFleur had never heard before. It broke him out of his daze.

Nearly tripping on the corner of the bed as he ran toward the front of the boat, he cursed the bed, cursed the dim light, and as he fumbled for the latch on the small access door into the bow, cursed the boat, the builder of the boat, the boat dealer who had sold him the boat, and anyone who had ever had anything to do with this or any other boat.

"Goddam boats!"

The small door opened with a crash, slamming against the wall. Newton cowered on the bed, and then as LaFleur turned back to look for him, launched himself into the air and locked himself around LaFleur's neck, his claws digging into the detective's bare shoulders, his head tucked under LaFleur's chin as tightly as it would go.

"Hold on!" LaFleur told Newton, as he crawled through the access door into the small area in the bow, under the front deck. It was even darker in here, but LaFleur knew what he was looking for, and felt around above him until he felt the dogs on the bow hatch. He was up and out onto the bow in a few seconds. It was no longer dark; the exploding fuel tanks had taken off half the rear deck, and orange fire lit up the marina. Black smoke poured out of the rear compartment.

LaFleur crawled forward on his hands and knees, Newton clinging ever tighter. Neither one of them wanted to go into the water. Even in summer, the lake never got much warmer than sixty. And it was still dark. No, the water would not be good.

Just as he was about to give in to desperation and go overboard anyway, LaFleur saw an old iron ladder hanging off the side of the pier, just in front of the bow. He couldn't reach it from where he was. Carefully sliding over to the edge of the boat, LaFleur reached out and gave a hard jerk on the front line, nearly pulling his shoulder out of the socket. The boat didn't move. He reached out and yanked on the line again. Whether from his second effort, or due to chance, the boat drifted forward slowly. The ladder was now barely within reach. LaFleur sat up, swung his legs over the side, and then turned 180 degrees and lowered himself down the side of the boat, chest on the gunwale, stretching his legs out in the direction of the ladder. Newton reasserted his hold around LaFleur's neck, but didn't make a sound.

When he felt his left foot hit a rung, LaFleur stretched himself to the limit, and was able to hook the rung with his foot. Something blew up at the back of the boat, and the resulting swell rocked the boat slightly closer to the ladder. He grabbed the side of the ladder, twisted himself into position, turned his foot onto the top of the rung, and pulled himself onto the ladder, nearly falling into the dark water below him. Clutching the sides of the ladder as he caught his breath, he looked back at the boat. It was completely engulfed in flames by now, and already listing badly to port and stern. It would go down quickly from here.

He let go of the ladder with one hand just long enough to wipe the sweat out of his eyes, then started to climb. After just one step up, still below the edge of the dock, he stopped as his old instincts kicked in. If whoever blew up the boat was watching, they possibly thought him dead by now. Maybe he could use that to his advantage. If he could get out of here unseen, and remain out of sight for a few days, he could channel his rising anger into finding out who had done this to him.

He first scanned the other side of the marina behind him, then peered warily over the top of the ladder; no one in sight. Quickly running to cover at the side of the boathouse, he finally managed to get Newton uncurled from around his neck and cradled in his arms. He'd have scars on his shoulders.

From the end of the boathouse, he ran across the parking lot, ducking behind the boats trailered there, then across the open road—no avoiding it—to a row of bushes. From the cover of the hedgerow, he searched the area again to see if anyone might be hanging around watching, but still didn't see anyone. The boat was already more than half submerged; it wouldn't be long now. He heard sirens, and glimpsed red and blue flashing lights heading for the marina, just a few blocks away from the fire station.

Circling along the edge of the ballpark, he made his way to East Seventh, then headed downtown—Arlene's comic shop on Bridge was the closest "safehouse" he could think of at the moment.

"My God!"

Waking with a start, LaFleur saw Arlene looming over him. He had decided not to wake her up in the middle of the night—she and her husband Larry lived in the

134

apartment above the shop—and had instead very quietly broken in. He and Newton had curled up together behind the main display case.

"Good morning, Arlene," said LaFleur, as if there were nothing unusual about his being there.

Another "My God!" was all Arlene could muster.

As LaFleur slowly got up, back and ankles cracking loudly in protest, he motioned toward the back of the shop. "Sorry about the back door, Arlene; I'll get it fixed as soon as possible. You should invest in some better locks. Oh, and don't tell anyone I'm here, by the way."

She raised her hands in exasperation. "Are you going to tell me what you are doing here? And where are your clothes?"

"Well…you've heard the expression 'long story?'"

She sighed—she had long given up being surprised by anything LaFleur did—and started to lead him upstairs. Newton still cowered behind the display case. LaFleur picked him up and followed Arlene up the stairs.

Sitting at the kitchen table, dressed in a set of Larry's work clothes—a tight fit, but better than nothing, and LaFleur was certainly not going to look a gift horse in the mouth—he told them what had happened as briefly as he could. Arlene made breakfast, unable to stop shaking her head in disbelief. Larry took the news with his typical equanimity—he didn't fluster easily, which confirmed for LaFleur that he'd made the right choice in coming here. LaFleur had already called Maggie to let her know he was all right—the story was sure to be on the local news—and asked her to call both Michael and Father Tommy. He was anxious, to say the least, to talk to both of them, now that things had suddenly escalated to a new level. It was no longer a matter of casual interest.

135

Father Tommy called back less than five minutes later, and said he was on his way over. Michael had not called yet. Maggie called, saying that she still hadn't been able to get in touch with Michael; she didn't have his cell number. LaFleur started to say he had the number programmed in his phone, hang on a minute, then realized where he was, and where his phone was. In the muck. Maggie said she'd call the hospital and track him down.

"I even had security cameras running," LaFleur explained to the group, "but fat lot of good it did—anything we might have captured is gone now, sitting in the bloody muck at the bottom of the marina."

"Just call Blueray," Arlene said. "He's got it."

"What?"

"The video stream from your CCTV cameras. Blueray told me all about it. He's been capturing everything remotely."

It was LaFleur's turn to shake his head. "I'll be damned. Kid's a bloody genius."

Thirty minutes later, Father Tommy, LaFleur, and Arlene were huddled around Arlene's laptop; Larry had gone to work, and they still hadn't heard anything from Michael. Blueray was on the VOIP "phone" link guiding them though the process of viewing the files he'd saved from the night before.

After fast-forwarding through long empty periods, nothing but gulls strolling around—though there was one unexpected cormorant that happened by—someone finally appeared on the dock and went into the boat. This happened at about ten p.m., Blueray said. LaFleur had been at Patz at that hour, on his way home from the hospital. He'd stopped in to ask—discreetly—if Pat or Pat knew anything about Nikki's past ordeal. They both said they'd never heard anything about it, from Nikki or anyone else.

Blueray backed up the video image so they could watch as the person approached the boat, but the night vision capabilities of the cameras were only marginal; they could tell only that someone of small stature had gone into the boat and that they were carrying something. There was no evidence of whoever it was having any difficulty getting in. Switching to the interior video stream provided the answer. It was Nikki.

"Hell's bells," LaFleur exclaimed. "Only Nikki. Okay, Blueray, stop it there." The image froze; Nikki was in the process of setting a large grocery bag on the galley counter. "Let's go back to the external camera and keep going ahead. Someone else must have come later."

"I don't know, A.C.," said Father Tommy hesitantly. "Shouldn't we go ahead and watch what she does?"

"Hell, I think she's just making a delivery for me. Snacks and stuff for the poker game tomorrow," he clarified for Arlene. "Um, today. Guess that'll have to wait."

"I still think we should make sure," Tommy said.

LaFleur shrugged, telling Blueray to go ahead and take it off pause. "If you insist, Padre."

They watched as Nikki set the bag down on the counter, and noticed that she had actually brought in two bags; the other, smaller bag was sitting on the floor next to her feet. After putting what LaFleur guessed was the bag of sandwiches in the refrigerator, Nikki picked up the other bag and disappeared from view. She was only gone for about two minutes, then appeared briefly just at the edge of the camera's range as she left the boat. Blueray immediately switched to the external view, locating the right segment quickly, and they saw Nikki walk off down the dock. She wasn't carrying anything as she left.

"See that?" Tommy asked. "What happened to the other bag she was carrying?"

"Hell, I don't know. Probably something else I asked her to bring over. Must have left it over on the table."

The Father looked dubious. "Maybe. I guess we can ask her."

"Sure, you, or Michael, even better, he can just ask her. Okay, Blueray, let's look outside again, from this point on."

Nothing appeared; the camera just showed an empty dock, the image sometimes slowly drifting up and down as the boat rocked. "Is it running?" asked LaFleur. "What time are we up to?"

"About one a.m.," said Blueray.

They continued to watch the empty dock. Nothing bigger than a moth appeared in view of the camera until the image started bouncing all over the place, then finally went black.

"That's it?" LaFleur asked anxiously. "That's the end? What time is that, Blueray?"

"Just after two."

"But that doesn't make any sense. Why don't we see whoever it was who came to the boat later?"

"Aren't you ignoring the evidence?" Tommy asked. "It's on the video. Nikki is the only one who came to the boat."

"Yes, I guess so," LaFleur said reluctantly. "That's certainly what the raw data shows—Nikki was apparently the only one there. So I agree we can't ignore that, but we've still got to interpret it correctly. And we don't know what happened before we started running the video surveillance. The day Randall was at Patz, for example. He could have planted something days ago. Nikki coming to the boat might be just a coincidence."

"You could be right," Tommy said, though LaFleur heard the doubt in his voice. "We really, really need to talk to Nikki."

"And to Randall." LaFleur looked back at the computer. "Uh, Blueray—I guess that's all we need for now. And thanks. You're a genius."

"No problem, Detective. Let me know if you need anything else." The window Blueray had displayed on Arlene's computer disappeared as he said goodbye and cut the audio connection as well.

"Damn it all, where's Michael?" asked LaFleur. "We need to work out a plan here; I can't be seen in public until we figure out what the bloody hell is going on."

Michael was at that moment standing in shocked disbelief behind the police barricades at the dock where LaFleur's houseboat used to be, watching fire department divers bring up scraps of debris. They had not located the body, someone in the crowd told him.

He'd figured it out too late.

As he was turning away, wondering what to do next, his iPhone rang.

"Come to Arlene's right away," he heard Father Tommy say, before he could even say hello.

"What—"

"Don't say anything. LaFleur's here."

The phone bounced when it hit the ground. *Good thing I just put the new case on it*, he thought, distractedly. He picked up the phone and ran to the car.

CHAPTER 23

When Michael first came in and saw LaFleur, standing at Arlene's kitchen table with Father Tommy, he could hardly speak. Then the three of them whooped it up, hugging and slapping shoulders, shaking hands.

Once things calmed down, LaFleur asked Arlene if they could have some privacy—he had some things to tell Michael and the Father that he wanted to keep among just the three of them for now. As she was late opening the store anyway, Arlene left them at the kitchen table.

As soon as they heard Arlene opening up downstairs, LaFleur turned to Michael.

"I got some information concerning Nikki yesterday," he began, "and it's not nice."

"But I've got something I have to tell you about Nikki first," Michael replied. "That's why I went to the marina this morning, I was frantically trying to find you; you

140

weren't answering your phone—as usual, I thought then—but I was too late. She'd already gotten to you. Or so I thought."

"What the hell are you talking about, already gotten to me? All she did was deliver the stuff for the game. We saw her on the video, Blueray showed it to us this morning, he'd been streaming it remotely. I thought it'd all gone down with the boat. So, anyway, it must have been someone earlier, Randall, probably, or—"

"Hold on. You saw Nikki? On the boat?"

"Yeah. Like I said, she delivered the sandwiches, put them in the fridge, then left. No big deal."

Michael rubbed his face and sighed with fatigue. "We were in bed the other night—no, just listen for a second—and she was acting a little strange. First, she wouldn't let me—uh, pardon me, Father, but—"

"Don't worry, Michael. You can't say anything I haven't heard in confession a million times or more."

"Yeah, I guess. Anyway, she wouldn't take off her nightie, or teddy, or whatever they call it, a silk thing, just a skimpy little Victoria's Secret kind of thing, you know? She kept it on the whole time that we—well, made love," he said, glancing guiltily at Father Tommy, who just nodded. Michael paused. "And then afterwards, she started prying into what the three of us—you, me and the Father—were doing together, never quite asking right out, but hinting a lot about the fires. Obviously she'd been overhearing things from us at Patz, and it was like she was trying to get me to tell her what we had found out. And if there were still official investigations going on."

"I don't see what you're getting at. So she was curious. So are a lot of people."

"I'm getting to that. She somehow knew about your meeting with the arson investigator, for example, and seemed really interested in that. And I told her some of what we'd been working on, about the photos we'd been looking at. When I told her we'd been using special software to do facial recognition of the crowds at several of the fires, she got kind of agitated."

"Agitated? How?"

"Nervous. Jumpy. We'd been lying there pretty relaxed for awhile, sort of even getting back into the mood again, when she started asking me about the fires. When I told her about the photos, she got up and left the room for a few minutes. Still wearing the teddy around her waist—she never would take it off, even when—but I've gotten off track. When we were lying there, the first time, and were, well, getting serious? I glimpsed something small and dark on her back, down low, right above her—in the small of her back. I couldn't see the whole thing, but it was a tattoo."

LaFleur sat back in exasperation. "Okay, I get that she was acting maybe a little too curious about what we've found out about the fires. Guess we weren't—I wasn't—as careful as I should have been, talking about some of it. And you were a little careless, too, telling her about the photo imaging, but we've never really found anything concrete there, right? And now it's all in the mud anyway, and what's that got to do with a tattoo on Nikki's back? Plenty of girls have them these days."

"Not like this." LaFleur didn't comment. "So, like I told you," Michael said, "I didn't see the whole thing, it was partially covered by the Victoria's Secret thingy. It looked like foreign language characters, and a pattern of some kind. At first I thought it was some kind of good luck character, with flowers or butterflies, or something. It was kind of dark, and I was preoccupied. I didn't realize what it was until this morning, when I woke up from a nightmare and knew exactly what it was." LaFleur and Tommy looked at one another as Michael paused again.

"And?" Tommy finally asked.

"The pattern I saw wasn't flowers or butterflies, it was flames," Michael said grimly. "And the characters? They were Greek. 'Pi' and 'rho,' as a matter of fact."

Obviously the implications would not yet be clear to Tommy, as he said, "Huh? The Greek characters you'd found in the photos, the ones you told me about the other day?"

LaFleur's expression told Michael that he had realized immediately what the tattoo could mean. But before he could say anything, Michael continued.

"Yeah. That's right, Father. The 'pyro' graffiti tag. And if you'll think back on those photos, A.C., the woman's face, the one that got flagged as common in more than one of the photos? Looked a little like Nikki, wouldn't you say?"

A look of distressed resignation clouded LaFleur's face as he quickly began to assimilate what he knew about Nikki's assault with the information Michael had just revealed.

"Michael, what I have to tell you about Nikki, it has to do with Randall."

"I guessed as much," Michael said. "She told me about it."

"About the rape? The burns?"

The look on Michael's face told LaFleur that Nikki had apparently not told Michael quite everything. The Father gasped.

143

"Michael," said LaFleur steadily, "I think we have a problem."

They were interrupted by Arlene hollering up the stairs at them.

"Hey, guys? I don't know if this is important or not, but Nikki's across the street. Just standing there. Shall I call her over?"

The answer "No!" was given in three-part unison.

It didn't take LaFleur long to fill them in on what he'd learned from Dr. Vito Martin. Figuring out exactly what it meant was going to take a little bit longer.

***

"No, I don't think that's a good idea."

"What other choice do we have?"

"We have all kinds of choices."

"What, like 'do nothing' is a choice?"

"I didn't say that."

"You obviously can't stay here."

"I agree."

"What about Nikki? We've got to do something, confront her somehow, get her to—"

"We don't have any proof."

"Exactly."

"She might lead us to the killer."

"Or, she might—"

"We need to flip this thing around, one way or the other."

"Maybe can draw her out. Get her into a neutral space, negotiate, find out what she's up to—"

"What are you talking about, Father? She tried to kill him."

144

"We don't know that, not for sure."

"We have to know."

"Michael, can you arrange to meet with her?"

"Not now. Not after what happened."

"No, I suppose not. Any other ideas? Padre?"

"Like I was trying to say. The church. Maybe we can, oh, I don't know, lure her there. She would feel safe there."

"Safe? Even if we could get her to come to the church, why would that make any difference?"

"She's a Catholic."

"So was Torquemada."

"Listen, A.C., we've got to get you out of here, no matter what. We shouldn't involve Arlene and Larry any more than we already have, and—"

"I don't know, it seems—"

"Come to the church. She'll follow."

"What do we expect to get from her if and when she shows up?"

"Just what we've been talking about. She obviously knows something, or has some other reason to be following you; we've got to find out what that is. I don't know any way to do that other than to confront her, but in a place where we have some control."

"Hmmm. Okay. Let's try it. I can't think of anything else. You, Michael?"

"Don't we need a 'Plan B?'"

"Plan B is to come up with a better plan."

"What about a way to monitor the church, the way you did the boat?"

"We don't have time for anything that sophisticated."

"Okay, then, maybe post a watch?"

"No, that's not necessary. The Padre and I can handle whatever happens, I'm sure."

"If you say so."

"Okay, then. Let's do it. When?"

"The sooner the better."

"How long will it take you to bring your car around?"

"Ten minutes."

"Okay. Michael, you just go home and wait to hear from us."

"Okay. I'll keep my phone on."

"Absolutely. And Padre, stay close to me."

"Don't worry, I'll be there with you, or right next door."

"Okay."

"Are you ready?"

"Yeah."

"Okay. Guess we'll just have to play this by ear."

"Yeah. See you in a few minutes."

CHAPTER 24

Arranging the Father's bivouac equipment in a small storage closet under the bell tower stairs, LaFleur started to feel as if he really was up on a mountain side somewhere, clinging dearly for his life.

They had not seen Nikki as they left Arlene's, but Tommy was confident that she'd follow. He'd waited at the church with LaFleur for several hours; LaFleur finally convinced him that if Nikki was going to come at all, it would probably be the next day. Tommy went to the rectory to get a few hours sleep, promising he'd be back by dawn. He was still convinced that Nikki would not be able to resist the chance to confront LaFleur—why else had she tracked him to Arlene's?—and was equally sure that the Church provided the perfect opportunity for finding some sort of resolution. Michael, though still slightly shell-shocked by the details of Nikki's abuse, had also finally agreed that trying to get her engaged somehow was worth a try. As a plan, it sucked. But they all felt they had little choice.

Unable to sit up any longer, LaFleur was just settling down onto his sleeping pad when he heard a noise in the sacristy. He quickly got up and switched off the closet light. Standing there in the dark, he was unavoidably reminded of the last night on the boat.

"Padre?" he called, optimistically. *No, he should still be sleeping.*

All he got in answer was a clattering sound, as if someone had knocked something over in the small adjoining room.

He crept out into the bell tower. There was no light showing under the sacristy door. He fumbled for the switch on his flashlight. Opened the sacristy door slowly. Raised the flashlight and started panning the beam slowly across the room.

"Hello, Mr. LaFleur," he heard Nikki say. "I thought you'd be asleep by now."

The flashlight jerked toward the sound of her voice, lighting her up like a Halloween party-goer. In spite of the warm weather, she was wearing a long trench coat, one arm crossed in front of her, giving her an even more sinister look.

"Ah. Nikki. We hoped you'd decide to, uh, visit. We need to talk."

"Talk? Oh, I suppose we can talk for a few minutes. But I really don't have a lot of time. There's something I have to do."

"It was you? The boat?"

Shifting something under her coat, Nikki moved closer. LaFleur kept the light on her.

"Of course it was me. I had to stop you from interfering."

"I can think of better ways…"

"No, this is really the only way," she replied, pulling a red, one-gallon can out from under her coat. "I've waited a long time; I'm not going to pass up the opportunity." She unscrewed the cap and motioned towards the door to the bell tower while moving even closer. LaFleur smelled gasoline. "Out," she commanded.

Backing out through the door, LaFleur tried to remember the layout of the tower room, planning an exit. Where was the outside door, and how was it latched? It had a bar across it, he suddenly remembered.

After closing the sacristy door behind them, Nikki quickly inserted herself between LaFleur and the exterior door, adapting her plan to the new circumstance of finding LaFleur awake. She looked around the bell tower, noting the camping gear in the storeroom. "Nice place you've got here," she said without humor. She looked over at the stairs leading up the side of the tower wall to the belfry above. A lower set of steep steps led to a horizontal platform that crossed over from one side of the tower to the other, about sixty feet above them. From there a narrower set of steps was attached to the wall and led to a trapdoor in the floor of the belfry itself. Nikki continued directing LaFleur, forcing him to the stairway leading up to the tower itself. He prepared to rush her.

"Up the stairs." She now held a butane lighter in one hand, gasoline in the other, and as she spoke, splashed some of the gas on the floor at LaFleur's feet.

LaFleur backed up onto the lower steps, holding out his hands. "Listen, Nikki, we can work through this." *God damn it, that sounded weak as hell.* "We know what happened. We can make sure he pays for what he did."

"People like him never pay for what they do to people like me," Nikki snapped. "You should know that. The only way he'll pay—the same way the others *should* have paid—is if I do it. But this time it will be certain. And permanent. And I have been waiting for years. You cannot stop me."

Others.

"How many fires have you started, Nikki? At least three fraternity fires over the years, right? And the pizza parlor in '98? Fortunately no one was killed in those, though it was close, and much to your regret, it seems. And haven't you been just a little indiscriminate? Someone did finally die in one of your fires," he said, sure now that the fire that killed Amy was her work. "Was that just another sick attempt to get to the fraternity members living in the apartments above?" She flinched at this. "It was, wasn't it? But the fire was worse than you planned, and it was Amy Polwicz's bad luck to have been there instead. Don't you even care that you murdered an innocent young girl?"

Nikki's shoulders slumped and her voice dropped to nearly a whisper. "Yes, of course I care. That will be taken care of tonight, too."

She straightened and advanced with the can held out in front of her. "Up the stairs, Mr. LaFleur." She looked up. "To that platform," she said, raising the lighter to indicate the wooden walkway high above them, at the top of the first set of stairs. "Now! Do it!"

"Nikki. Don't. We can take care of this. It's not too late."

"It was always too late, LaFleur. Up!" Nikki poured the rest of the gasoline out onto the dilapidated wood as

150

LaFleur climbed to the platform. She backed away from the bottom of the stairway, leaving a trail of gasoline to the sacristy door, then threw the can to the other side of the room. It landed on the cement floor with a loud ringing clatter that echoed up the bell tower.

Nikki opened the door and stepped into the sacristy, then turned and bent down with the lighter. "I'm sorry," she said, as she touched the flame to the floor.

The fire reached the base of the stairway before she even got the door closed behind her.

For the second time in as many days, LaFleur faced the terrifying prospect of burning to death. *At least Newton is safe at Arlene's this time.*

The old wood was tinder-box dry and the fire spread quickly. In just minutes, as LaFleur stood watching helplessly, flames were leaping up to within a few feet of the platform where he now stood. He tried to make his way back down the stairs, hoping to get close enough to the floor to jump, but only got a couple of feet before the heat and smoke drove him back up. He looked down at the concrete floor, gauging how badly he'd be hurt if he jumped. *Probably kill me*, he thought, *but then again, what do I have to lose?*

Trying not to panic, he looked around desperately for another option. The stone wall ran unchecked all the way to the floor; there was no way down other than the stairway. He looked up and saw the same unbroken wall of stone rising above him, all the way to the top of the tower. Then he saw the trapdoor in the belfry floor.

He could sound an alarm.

CHAPTER 25

Nikki was crying as she ran out of the church. *Stupid old man.* She hated having to do that, but she'd had no choice. It really was too late.

She ran to a hedge at the edge of the churchyard and retrieved a large backpack, then made her way down the hill towards town, using alleys and small dark streets, carefully staying out of sight, moving with quick determination.

By the time she reached the Pi Rho Delta house, just a few blocks away, she was no longer crying. She had a look of cold hatred on her face, the look LaFleur had glimpsed at Patz when Randall walked in and surprised her. Carefully avoiding the outdoor spotlights, Nikki walked quickly to the back of the building and entered through the back door she'd jimmied earlier. She'd also taken care of the light over the door. The house was closed for the summer, so it had been easy to set this up.

Once inside, she went through to the kitchen, which was located in the rear at the other side of the darkened house. Here she carefully set the backpack down near a large pantry on one side of the kitchen. From there she went back to the main foyer and up the large entry stairs, down a long hallway and into a large bedroom.

Randall had regained consciousness.

Fortunately, she had taken the precaution of also gagging him. His eyes followed her as she moved to the side of the bed, but he didn't make a sound.

It had been pure hell getting him here. How she'd gotten away with it with no one seeing her, she didn't know. She'd dropped him off the edge of the tailgate while trying to get him into the back of her old Toyota pickup and was afraid he'd broken his neck. That would have been very unsatisfying. But he was okay. The old carpet she'd wrapped him up in must have cushioned the fall.

She pulled a chair up from the corner behind her and sat down wearily.

"You don't know how much trouble you've caused me," she said. "But it won't be long now."

Randall struggled with the ropes binding his wrists and ankles to the bed posts, but he could barely move; she'd trussed him up tightly while he had been under. A bottle of ether and a rag sat on a small bedside table.

Nikki opened her mouth as if to continue, but then just sat back and closed her eyes. *This could even be the room where it happened,* she thought with a sudden chill.

Randall started to whimper.

Nikki didn't move.

CHAPTER 26

Standing on the platform, LaFleur looked around for the pull rope he thought should be hanging down to the room below; he finally spied it, running down the other side of the tower, totally out of reach. He'd have to get into the belfry.

He frantically crawled up the last set of steps. When he got to the door, he reached up with one arm and pushed.

The trapdoor didn't budge.

LaFleur braced himself with his knees against the edge of the ladder-like stairs and reached up to try again, this time with both palms flat against the splintered wood. The door creaked slightly.

The smoke was getting thicker, making LaFleur's eyes water and causing him to cough harshly. He looked again for any kind of handle or latch that could be holding it closed from the outside. Nothing.

He climbed one step higher and put his shoulder against the door, precariously balanced and gripping the edge of the stairs tightly. He could feel the door bow under the pressure.

When the door finally flew open, he barely kept from falling, hitting the back of his head squarely against the edge of the opening just as he caught himself. He reached up through the opening and pulled himself up into the belfry, cursing all the way.

"Bloody hell, Padre, doesn't anyone ever come up here?" he said, his voice echoing in the dark chamber.

Even in the dim light coming in through the arched, decorated windows on every side, he could tell that the bell didn't get many visitors. It was streaked with bird dung, and the floor was thick with dust. He started coughing even harder.

Stumbling in the half light as smoke poured in through the open trap door, LaFleur groped his way around the edge of the belfry. Passing by the west side window, he suddenly caught a glimpse of Oswego Hospital on the hill across the river. He couldn't help but think of Angie, the nurse who had died there under suspicious circumstances so many years ago, and the resulting attempt on Maggie's life, just last year. The image of Maggie, lying on the E.R. floor gasping for breath, lungs paralyzed by curare, flashed though his mind. Along with the image came a brief surge of panic as he realized he might be the one gasping for air this time.

He had to ring the bell. He kicked it and it returned a sad, muffled gong, hardly enough to scare a bird, much less raise outside attention. Feeling his way carefully around the framework holding the bell—it was as big as he was—he came to a large iron wheel, at least six feet in diameter. It looked like it was attached to some sort of mechanism below the bell; there was a chain, like a giant bicycle chain, running around the top of the wheel and into the framework below.

LaFleur reached above his head, grasped the wheel with both hands, and gave a hard pull. The bell barely moved, as his hands slipped around the wheel, ripping the flesh on his hands. He wiped his palms on his pants, wincing. He didn't have enough energy left to curse.

Crawling back to the trapdoor, he looked down into the room below. The fire had reached the platform halfway up the tower, and so had slowed somewhat, but still inched steadily across the planks. *Always burning my bridges behind me somehow*, he thought. While he watched, the lower stairway broke loose and collapsed into a dramatic heap of sparks and ash on the tower floor. The fire would reach the final stairway before too much longer.

"Nothing to be done for it," he said. He went back to the wheel and grabbed onto it as tightly as he could. He pulled himself off of the floor, putting his whole weight against it, feeling the chain cut into his hands.

The bell rang. This time it was much more than a dull thud. It was bone-shaking, ear-splitting—and gratifying. He rang it again. Blood poured down his wrists and arms. He managed to ring it once more before he collapsed on the floor, coughing, bleeding, and smiling. Maybe he'd live.

***

Father Tommy woke up at about two a.m. He stared up into the darkness for a few seconds, as if trying to remember where he was. There was something he had to do...

156

Awake now, he swung his legs over the edge of the bed and sat up. What was it?

Pulling on shorts and a t-shirt, he went out into the rectory yard. Looked up at the sky. Went around to the side of the church. Saw smoke pouring from the belfry.

Dear God.

He ran to the bell tower. The outer door was locked—barred from the inside, he recalled. He ran to the front of the church and threw open the wide front doors.

Running down the aisle between the pews, he smelled the smoke. When he got to the door to the sacristy, his only access to the bell tower, it was locked.

"Dear God," he whispered again.

There was a large wooden chair sitting in the chancel. He picked it up and threw it against the door, which burst open with a crash.

He could scarcely believe what he saw as he stepped over the wreckage of the chair and into the tower. The lower stairway was nearly gone, a flaming heap on the floor in its place; the high horizontal platform was also burning, with the fire about half way to the steps up to the belfry. The door to the storage closet was hanging open. No LaFleur. Smoke and flames engulfed the interior of the tower, rushing up to the belfry. The tower was acting like a gigantic chimney.

"LaFleur!" he screamed.

"Up here!' came a faint reply.

As Tommy looked up, he saw LaFleur's head pop into view at the trapdoor opening.

"Padre! Up here!" LaFleur called, loudly this time.

"Hang on!" Tommy yelled back.

Dear God, dear God, dear God—this was the only prayer Tommy had at the moment, and he kept repeating it, *sotto voce*, over and over, as he quickly gathered up the gear he needed. A coil of rope slung over his shoulder. Slings. Quickdraws. Carabiners.

He quickly rigged a "diaper harness" around his waist, the simplest style—inelegant but effective, just three loops formed from a long, single loop of webbing, pulled around from each side and up between his legs, clipped together in front with a single carabiner. He ran to the climbing wall and grabbed the first handhold, pulling himself up off of the floor. A flaming board fell from somewhere above him and hit the floor in a shower of sparks.

At forty feet he stopped to catch his breath. He had never climbed the wall totally free like this, unroped, with no protection. If he fell he'd probably be killed. Not to mention the growing fire. The smoke was swirling around him, making his eyes burn. He looked up to make sure LaFleur was still up there, and that the fire hadn't advanced too far. LaFleur was there, head hanging out over the trapdoor opening, watching him climb. Tommy figured he had bare minutes before the fire got to the belfry steps.

"Padre!" LaFleur called. "Hurry!"

Tommy looked up and gave LaFleur a "thumbs up." He refrained from yelling back—*what do you think I'm doing?*

Sweat was pouring down Tommy's face and running into his eyes. He swiped his forehead with the back of his hand and kept climbing. His arms ached. His back ached. The smoke increased, making it almost impossible to see to the top of the tower. And it was getting hotter. His hands were sweating now too, and he lost his grip on a hold, catching himself only with great difficulty, and great pain, feeling his fingernails bend and break in a crack in the wall he'd somehow managed to wedge his fingers into. He didn't dare let go.

158

The wall had not been designed as a free climbing wall. Hanging precariously with one hand gripping a tiny hanger, the other still wedged into the crack, he scrabbled at the wall below him with the side of his foot, desperately trying to get a foothold on the edge of a stone.

He found a small foothold. As he pushed himself up, he reached up blindly, groping for the next handhold. His outstretched hand grasped only empty air, rough stone. There were no more handholds. No more hangers. The route he'd laid out veered to the left here. He could climb no higher. He was still about three feet below the walkway.

***

Nikki woke with a start to the sound of a church bell. *That crafty old devil.* She didn't have much time. "It sounds like LaFleur might save himself a second time," she said. "Well, I hope so."

She settled back in her chair, looking down at Randall with contempt. "You didn't even see me the other day at Patz, did you?" she asked Randall. He rolled his eyes wildly and struggled vainly against his bonds.

"Do you ever even think of me? At all? Are you ever— *sorry*—for what you and your friends did to me?"

Randall blinked hard several times. She didn't know if he was trying to answer in some kind of pathetic blinking code, or was just fatigued and dry-eyed. No matter.

"Christ, I'm tired," she said. Her head drooped.

CHAPTER 27

Tommy downclimbed as slowly as he could, back to the last hanger. He called up to LaFleur as he anchored himself in below the ledge. "You'll have to climb down to me!"

LaFleur nodded, then disappeared. A few seconds later, Tommy saw him lower himself backwards through the trapdoor and onto the stairs, then start climbing down slowly.

"Come down to the walkway," Tommy called up. LaFleur looked back over his shoulder and nodded again. He was moving slowly, Tommy saw, using his wrists rather than his hands to steady himself. As LaFleur climbed down, Tommy pulled the coil of rope up over his head, tied it off, and let it uncoil to the floor. He then looped it through the carabiner at his waist in a simple knot called a Munter Hitch. This would allow him to control his rappel down the wall. Now he just had to figure out how to get LaFleur down along with him.

Once LaFleur got down to the bottom of the upper stairs, Tommy saw LaFleur's bloody hands. They looked like the hands of fanatic penitents, the ones who self-inflicted stigmata, nailed their own hands to a board and had their friends carry them up a dusty street. The platform was burning about two feet away from LaFleur by now.

"Okay," Tommy called, as LaFleur carefully settled himself onto the walkway, "I'm going to throw you a harness." LaFleur nodded in assent, and Tommy carefully tossed up a long loop of webbing with a carabiner attached. LaFleur caught it with one hand, then looked down to Tommy for instructions. "Loop it around your waist so the two ends come together," Tommy called up, "then pull it up from the back, under your crotch." He watched in frustration as LaFleur fumbled with the webbing. "No!" Tommy yelled. "A loop from each side, and one between your legs! Look at mine!"

LaFleur looked down but could barely see Tommy through the thickening smoke. He was finally able to make out how Tommy's harness was configured, and saw what he was doing wrong; he had tried to loop it around his legs. He quickly redid the loops correctly and clipped the webbing together in front with the carabiner.

"Okay, that's it!" Tommy hollered in relief. Now he'd be able to clip into LaFleur's harness and guide him down, a much safer method. He hadn't wanted to take the chance of LaFleur falling while attempting a free rappel, with no harness and no way to control his descent. "Now you're going to have to somehow lower yourself over the edge of the walkway, down to me! Then I'll be able to clip into your harness."

Again there was only a nod of assent from LaFleur as they each positioned themselves. Tommy leaned out away from the wall, supported by the rope now looped through his carabiner, and reached up toward LaFleur. As LaFleur carefully edged himself over the side of the boardwalk, his legs dangled freely, his feet stretching involuntarily into mid-air trying to find a footing that didn't exist.

"Keep coming!" Tommy yelled.

Hanging off the ledge at armpit level, LaFleur yelled back over his shoulder. "That's as far as I can go!"

Tommy shook his head. "You'll have to drop lower. I can't reach you yet!"

LaFleur didn't move.

Tommy leaned out a bit further, angling over to LaFleur at the same time. "Drop down to me!"

Looking back again over his shoulder, LaFleur saw Tommy's looking up at him, eyes red from the smoke and shining with adrenaline. LaFleur slowly inched his elbows out straight along the edge of the wooden walkway. He remained motionless for a few seconds, then pushed himself off. He caught the edge of the platform with his hands at the last second, barely breaking his fall. He was hanging right next to Tommy now.

"Can you hold on while I get you clipped in?" Tommy yelled.

"Yeah." *Maybe*

Tommy reached over and clipped himself to LaFleur's harness with a quickdraw, a simple sling with pre-attached carabiners—not the thing he would have preferred to use, but it would work.

"Okay! Got you!" Tommy yelled excitedly. They were now attached at the hip, LaFleur's harness clipped to Tommy's, LaFleur still hanging by his hands. "Now, we're going to rappel down," Tommy told LaFleur. "You know what that is?"

"Sure. Eiger Sanction and all that," LaFleur answered, breathing heavily. "Let's hurry."

"Right. After I pull you off, try to get your feet over to the wall and walk down with me. Here we go." Tommy grabbed LaFleur around the waist and pulled him off the ledge, taking his whole weight. It felt like it was going to pull them both off the wall, but he'd been prepared for it. "Okay, brace yourself against the wall with your feet!" he told LaFleur. "Then just let me take us both down. Don't worry if you can't stay on the wall!"

With one arm around LaFleur, the other on the rope, Tommy slowly guided their way down, essentially walking the wall. LaFleur ended up more or less just hanging from Tommy's side. Tommy lowered them to the ground as quickly as he could.

As their feet hit the floor, they heard sirens. Before they could unclip themselves, a fire ax splintered the tower door, and a fireman rushed in. As a draft of fresh air blew into the tower, the smoke at the floor cleared and fire roared up the stairway above them and into the belfry.

"Ah," said LaFleur. "In the nick of time." He hurriedly unclipped himself from Tommy and turned and ran out the door, still in his own harness, as Tommy watched in amazement. Tommy ran outside and called after him.

"A.C.! What are you doing?"

But LaFleur was already almost out of sight.

163

CHAPTER 28

The Pi Rho Delta house was dark when LaFleur arrived. Panting from the short run, he pulled hard on the front door handle, smearing it with blood. It was locked. He picked up a big rock from the edge of a flower bed and went to a large window next to the porch. Smashing the window out a section at a time, he soon had a hole in the window frame large enough to crawl through.

Once inside, he called out loudly. "Hello! Anyone here?" A large staircase led from the foyer to the upper floors. He ran up the first few steps, then stopped and called out again.

As he started back up the stairway, he heard the sound of footsteps; someone was moving around on the floor above him. He heard a door open, and the clatter of a person running down a flight of stairs. The sound was coming from the far end of the house, to his right.

Turning quickly, LaFleur leapt down the stairs to the main floor and looked around, trying to get his bearings. Another door slammed, now to his left. Moving as quickly as he could in the darkness, he made his way down a hallway toward the sound.

As he rounded a corner at the far end of the hallway, he saw light shining from under a door at the far end of the house. Quietly now, he crept toward the door, passing a narrow stairway at the end of the hall. He heard someone moving around as he pressed up against the door, easing it open. Through the crack he'd opened he saw the kitchen.

Nikki was standing across the kitchen with her back to him, near a large pantry. She turned when she heard LaFleur open the door the rest of the way. If she was surprised to see him, she didn't show it.

"You never give up, do you?" she said. A large black canvas pack sat on the floor at her feet.

"Nope." He moved carefully through the doorway into the large kitchen and stood behind a big steam table. "Not when there's still a chance."

"A chance for what?" she asked caustically. "Another chance to get yourself killed?"

"A chance at finding an answer. Finding a resolution. Justice, maybe."

Nikki's face clouded. She looked at the floor, at the bag lying there. "I told you, you don't even know what justice is," she mumbled.

He came slowly around to the front of the table, edging his way closer to her. He stopped when she suddenly looked up.

"Get back!"

"What are you doing here, Nikki?" he asked gently.

She knelt down on the floor and unzipped the pack.

"You just wouldn't let it go, would you, LaFleur? I mean, really. What is it with you, anyway?" She pulled a small glass jug out of the bag and set it carefully on the floor, then reached into the bag again and brought out a red gallon can. LaFleur recognized the can—it was just like the one she'd used at the church tower—but frowned in confusion at the glass jar.

"What's in the jar, Nikki?" *Try to keep her talking. Someone must be on their way here, right? Won't Padre know this is where I am?*

"Oh, yeah. You wouldn't know that, would you. No evidence left behind in your boat, was there?" She stood up, holding the gas can, then leaned over into the pantry, sloshing gasoline around on the shelves, walls, and floor. Then she poured the rest in a circle around her feet. She dropped the can.

LaFleur started toward her again, but she suddenly pulled a butane lighter out of her pocket and screamed "Get back!" at him again. He backed up a couple of steps, pressing his hands to the floor in a conciliatory gesture.

"Okay. But Nikki, listen to me. What do think this will accomplish? Burning down a fraternity house won't solve anything. What did any of your other fires result in, other than causing a lot of unnecessary pain and suffering, to people you didn't even know."

"I already told you, I'm sorry for that."

"Sorry? You think that's enough?"

"Of course not. I didn't say that." She knelt down to the floor and picked up the bottle. She held it up.

"Ether, LaFleur. You wouldn't have guessed that, would you?"

"Well, as a matter of fact, I did know about the ether, Nikki. I just didn't think it was you."

166

"No, damn right you didn't," she said. "You thought it was Randall, didn't you?" When he didn't answer, she screamed again, "DIDN'T YOU?"

"Yes, Nikki, I did. I thought it was Randall."

"Well, now you know. And like I said before, it's too late. You—I don't care about you anymore. You couldn't stop me before. You can't stop me now." She held the bottle higher.

"Nikki! Wait! What possible good is this going to do?"

"You wanted justice, didn't you? Well, DIDN'T YOU?"

He nodded, waiting for her to continue.

"Well, there's going to be justice here tonight, LaFleur. More justice than you could know. Do you know who's upstairs right now, in the room right above my head, tied to his bed?" LaFleur shook his head, no longer trusting himself to speak. "Lance Randall, LaFleur. Tied to his bed, unconscious, just like I was unconscious when he and his miserable friends raped me. Raped me and burned me, LaFleur." She waved the bottle back and forth as she ranted. "Ether, LaFleur. Neat stuff. Many uses. I'm putting what I learned in my chemistry class to good use, don't you think? The class I took with Lance Randall, as a matter of fact. What is that called, LaFleur? Irony? Is that what it is?"

"Nikki, please..." He edged closer to her.

"It's over, LaFleur," she said quietly. "Tonight, everyone pays." She flicked the trigger on the butane lighter and held the flame high.

"Everyone pays," she said again, even more softly this time, as she threw the glass bottle to the floor. It shattered instantly. She dropped the lighter to her side and the ether ignited with a low whooshing sound, like a short gust of wind. The gasoline caught a split second later.

167

Before LaFleur could react, a huge ball of fire engulfed Nikki where she stood, the flames reaching him as well. He felt the hair on the backs of his hands burn off. He involuntarily backed away, momentarily stunned at the sight of Nikki's clothing catching fire. Then her hair, hanging loosely around her face and on her shoulders, burst into flame.

"Nikki!" LaFleur lowered his head and tried to approach her, but the gasoline had flared too quickly, and the flames were too hot. He backed away again, eyebrows and arms singed, aghast at the sight of Nikki standing stock still in the middle of the fire, her eyes closed tightly in pain. The fire spread rapidly from the pantry to the ceiling. It would not take long for it to burn through to the floor above, LaFleur knew. Smoke began billowing throughout the room. He coughed and made his way back to the door on the other side of the kitchen, backing away, eyes on Nikki.

A few seconds later, as he watched in dazed horror, Nikki collapsed to the floor without making a sound.

The fire roared around her.

As he ran up the stairs, LaFleur heard sirens. Glancing out a window as he ran down the hall, he saw the pumpers pull up in front of the house, red and blue lights flashing, lighting up the hallway like dance floor strobes.

From Nikki's description, he knew the room where she had Randall tied up had to be at the end of the house, on the first floor, towards the back. He did not believe that the fire could have reached Randall yet, even as intense as it was.

He turned the corner at the end of the hall and ran to the rear of the house. He could see an open doorway about twenty feet in front of him. That must be it.

A blast of fire poured out of the open doorway just as he approached. Through the flames he could barely make out the form of Randall spread-eagled on a large bed in the middle of the room. Fire had already caught on the sheets hanging off the edge of the bed.

Nikki must have set some sort of fire bomb in the room, LaFleur realized belatedly.

He staggered back into the hall. His vision blurred. Someone called his name. He sank to his knees in shock and exhaustion, just as the firemen reached him.

Epilogue

"I can't believe I didn't see it sooner," said Michael.

He and Father Tommy were at a corner table at Patz, next to the windows. The weather had turned the last couple of days, and the harbor was clouded over by a light, misty rain. They stared morosely out at the river.

"And that all along, she was deceiving me…using me…" Michael continued, until his voice faltered. "Did A.C. tell you what they found in her apartment? All of the ether?" Tommy shook his head. "Cases of automotive starting fluid. Easy to get, and apparently relatively easy to condense out, using ice, or PVC pipe, or something. Along with a bottle she'd managed to buy from an online distributor, using a fake business name. There was even some tagged with a SUNY chemistry lab inventory label. Now that's ironic. And all just sitting there in her closet, while we…" He broke off.

Tommy nodded in sympathy. "Don't feel like you were the only one," he said. "She had us all fooled." He finished his beer and absentmindedly wiped his mouth with the back of his hand. "I wonder where those two are?" he said, referring to Maggie and LaFleur. "They should have been here long before now."

Michael turned and waved to the bartender, circling a hand to signal another round. The bartender nodded and called over the new waitress, Vicki. Michael had gasped in shock when he came in that afternoon and Pat introduced her—he thought he'd heard her say "Nikki."

"We just should have seen it," Michael repeated.

"I certainly don't blame you for not realizing sooner," Tommy answered. "None of us had any idea."

"Still, we never looked hard enough—never really looked—at the firesigns Nikki was giving," Michael said dejectedly. "LaFleur said it himself: she had the right signature, we just didn't look for it. We thought we had Randall's signature down, and that he fit the profile," he continued. "Everything—gender, age, opportunity, his trouble with the law, the shady business with Amy—it all fit. And Nikki...well, even if there were some signs, she was still an outlier."

"Yes, but what was it Debra Gallatin told LaFleur, only ten percent of arsonists are female?" said Tommy. "I don't think we could have known any sooner than we did, at least not by much."

"Yeah, I guess." Michael took a drink. "Hey, Father, what's the story about the bell? A.C. told me you never actually heard him ringing the church bell, is that right?"

"That's right. Never heard a thing. Didn't even know he'd rung the bell until he told me later, how he'd cut his hands up on the chain."

"Well, then, how did you know he was in trouble?"

"I just knew."

"You must have heard them subconsciously, in your sleep. That's the only rational explanation."

"Maybe," said Tommy slowly, obviously not agreeing. "Maybe. I prefer to think of it as divine intervention."

Vicki came up with the new round of drinks. "I heard what happened," she said tentatively, "with Nikki and all. I'm really sorry."

"Thanks, Vicki. Thanks a lot." Michael smiled at her. She ducked her head quickly and left. "Nice kid," he said, as she walked away.

Michael held up his glass. "Well, here's to…what shall we toast, Father? Justice?"

"Certainly. Why not?" Tommy replied, raising his glass. "To Justice."

Setting his glass down, Michael looked around to the entrance, as if expecting to see Maggie and LaFleur. "So LaFleur is moving in with Maggie, I hear."

"Yes, that's what they told me."

"Permanently?"

"Well, I think I would just say, 'indefinitely,'" Tommy said with a smile.

"Where *are* those two, anyway?"

***

Amy's headstone was polished pink granite, simply inscribed; no adornments, no flowers or angelic filigree. Just a few simple words.

"Amanda Polwicz -- Loving Daughter," it read, "June 10, 1990 - July 15, 2010."

Heads bowed, Maggie and LaFleur stood at the gravesite quietly. They were holding hands.

"Never knew her real name was 'Amanda,'" said LaFleur.

"Hmm, yes," said Maggie distractedly. "I think I saw that on her admittance papers."

LaFleur raised his head and looked around. "Angie's grave is just off over there," he said, motioning to the small hill to their right.

"I know," said Maggie.

"So, did I fail Amy, too?" asked LaFleur, "just like I failed Angie?"

"Oh, sweetheart, you didn't fail Amy. Or Angie."

"What about justice?"

"You've talked with Padre enough to know what his answer is," she said. He nodded. "Anyway," she said, "who's to say? Who is served? In this case in particular, we know who the victims are, and who's guilty."

LaFleur shuddered at a sudden thought: the famous photograph of the Buddhist monk who set himself on fire in the middle of Saigon years ago. He knew he'd never lose the image of Nikki standing in that kitchen as if in a trance, wrapped in flames. Burned into his memory, he reflexively thought, then shuddered again

"Is Nikki right now burning in hell, just like she burned here on earth a few days ago?" he asked.

"No," Maggie said forcefully. "I can't believe God would allow that."

"She was guilty, though."

"And she paid with her life. Deliberately, it seems. No, it was simply horrible circumstance and her inexpressible rage that drove her to act the way she did over all those years of setting fires. It's a wonder more people weren't hurt, or killed. Maybe she wasn't really trying to kill anyone, back then, maybe it was more a symbolic gesture; small fires she knew, or hoped, would do minimal damage." She turned and looked at LaFleur. "But I think the shock at suddenly seeing Randall in the bar, after all those years, triggered something else in her, something she'd obviously been repressing for a long time. Something ungodly, almost evil, in a way. I think Tommy would agree with me. Her tattoo—the flames, the pyromania characters, the link to the fraternity—and her previous arsons; all part of a desperate attempt on her part to somehow deal with the abuse she'd suffered.

"That could also explain her overreaction to what she saw as interference by you and Michael," she went on, "and her attempt to get you, especially, out of the way. Who knows, if you hadn't escaped, she might have gone after Michael next." She paused, reflecting on Nikki's last acts of vengeance. "She'd suddenly been confronted with, well, the 'opportunity' to avenge herself, and as she told you that night, A.C., she wasn't going to let you or anyone else stand in the way. No matter what the cost. Including her own life."

"And since New York is a death penalty state," said LaFleur, "maybe she figured she'd be executed eventually, anyway. Dying in the fire, she just accelerated that process." He turned away from Amy's grave, then hesitated.

"But what about Randall?" he asked. "He was guilty, too; not of murder, of course, but he did some pretty despicable things. And paid with his life as well. At Nikki's hand. Was that justice?"

"Nikki obviously thought so," said Maggie. She sighed. "You know, I can still see Amy's face, the night she was brought into the burn center. And to think that both Randall and Nikki—" She was unable to finish her thought. "I've given my notice at Clarke. I don't know how those nurses do it, year after year. I thought neonatal ICU was bad, but I'd even go back to that, rather than stay any longer at the burn unit."

"Well, I'll tell you," said LaFleur, "I sure thought I was going to end up in the burn unit myself. That's if I got out of the belfry at all, that is. I had a real flash of panic, wondering if I was going to die up there, looking out at the hospital where Angie died—where *you* almost died," he said, looking at Maggie intently, "due to my fumbling— now, wouldn't that have been perfect justice?"

"Listen to me, A.C.," Maggie said, just as intently. "Justice aside, you cared enough to try to do something about Amy's death. You cared, and you worked at it, and you tried to find...justice, truth, whatever...but the fact is that you did it, A.C., that you cared enough, and that's what is perfect about whatever justice there is in all of this, no matter what the outcome."

On the way out of the cemetery, LaFleur steered them past Angie's grave. They stood there silently for a minute or so, then LaFleur turned to Maggie, as if to say something, then stopped.

Maggie brushed a tear from his cheek and kissed him gently. She grabbed his hand.

"Come on," she said, coaxing him away. "We're late."

Acknowledgements

This book got its start on a long weekend in Oswego, with a group of literate and inventive friends and family sitting around the Fountain kitchen table: Sandy Fountain; Adrienne Abbott; Dr. Willie McLaughlin and Dr. Anne Seger; Jan and Phil Meyer; and Kurt "Chicken" Schmitt. John and Steve are willing to take all the blame from there.

In spite of a grueling college teaching schedule, Sarah Massey-Warren promptly reviewed every chapter and made consistently valuable suggestions. Extensive editing and proofreading services were provided by Debbie Abbott.

We are also indebted to a dedicated group of reviewers and advisors for their many excellent suggestions: Lisa Fountain MacFadden; Kurt Schmitt; Arlene Spizman; Sarah and Ron Uva; Shelley Proano; Pat Grulich; Christina Eccleston; and Delphine Winter. Mike Luckow provided much needed technical advice for the rock climbing scenes. Many thanks to all.

For their enthusiastic support and superb professional advice, and for providing a marvelous platform for our books, we thank Bill Reilly and Mindy Ostrow of the River's End Bookstore, located in downtown Oswego at 19 West Bridge Street. Visit them when you are in town, or online at http://www.riversendbookstore.com.

About the Authors

Dr. John Fountain provided anesthesiology services to Oswego Hospital for nearly twenty-five years. He now lives in Lake Placid, New York, and is Chief of Anesthesiology at Adirondack Medical Center. Always adventurous, after graduating from Wayne State University School of Medicine in Detroit, Michigan, John traveled overseas to do his initial residencies—he first spent two years in Dunedin, New Zealand, followed by two years in Perth, Scotland (where he met his wife, Sandy). He then returned to the U.S. to do a third residency in anesthesiology in Lexington, Kentucky. John is an avid tennis player, skier, and as anyone who knows him can tell you, a fine storyteller.

Steve Abbott is a Colorado native, and lives in Boulder, Colorado with his wife Adrienne, and a cat, Melinda. He graduated from the University of Colorado, where he and John were roommates during their undergraduate years. He recently retired from his job at a large software company, and is happily pursuing other interests, including writing, playing the hammered dulcimer, and tournament poker. This is his and John's second collaboration.

6661764R0

Made in the USA
Charleston, SC
20 November 2010